TABLE OF CONTENTS

The Snare Drum

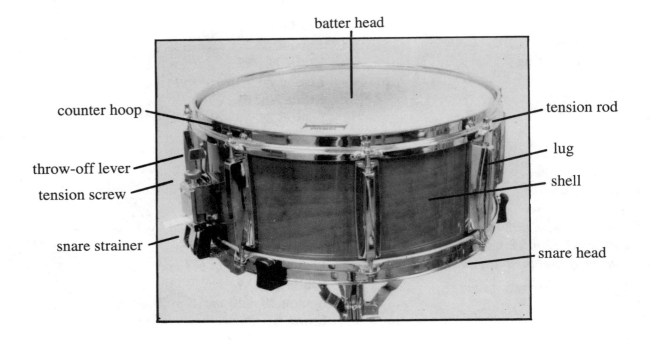

Playing Techniques

There are two methods of holding snare drum sticks: The traditional grip and the matched grip. Both are acceptable grips and are used by professionals in all styles of drumming. The traditional grip is a hold over from the days when drums were hung from the shoulders by slings. The angle of the drum dictated that the left hand be held in such a way as to get around the top of the drum. Within the past twenty years there has been great interest and popularity in the matched grip. There are numerous advantages inherent in this technique, particularly with beginning students.The most significant advantage comes from the ability to produce an even sound from both hands, something that concert snare drum playing demands. Numerous factors are involved in producing an even sound, including using a pair of drumsticks that are equal in pitch, a drum head that is evenly tuned, and a playing position on the head where both sticks are equidistant from the rim.

The matched grip is a perfectly natural manner of playing. If one holds his/her hands straight out from the body, one will notice a natural curve between the thumb and index finger. This natural curve remains present in a properly held drumstick. The player should grasp the stick approximately 1/3 the distance from the butt end between the thumb and index finger directly behind the thumb nail and at the first joint of the first finger. This is the "fulcrum" and is the point where slight pressure may be applied. The other fingers are lightly wrapped around the stick and are used to guide it while playing. The palms are down and the thumbs are in. The drumsticks are held at a 90° angle to one another. Both sticks are held identically. (See photo no. 1)

Another advantage of teaching and playing the matched grip is its immediate transferability to the other areas of percussion. One can play multiple percussion, drum set, and mallet-keyboard instruments with relatively the same hand position. Timpani can be played with a slight moderation in the technique.

Photo No. 1

With the traditional grip, the right stick is held identical to the matched grip. The left stick is held in the following manner: 1) Hold the stick securely in the crevice between the thumb and first finger 1/3 the distance from the butt of the stick. This is the fulcrum; 2) Bring the little finger and ring finger under the stick and rest the stick between the first and second joints of the ring finger; 3) Place the first two fingers lightly over the top of the stick. The left hand turns in a rotary motion similar to the turning of a door knob. (See photo no. 2) This grip is very popular in corps style drumming due to its visual possibilities not possible with the matched grip. Many jazz drummers prefer this grip due to its tonal possibilities at the drum set.

The snare drum should be positioned at a height and distance that will enable the player to remain in a relaxed position at all times. The drum should be approximately waist high and at a distance of 6" - 8" from the player, allowing the elbows to stay even with the side of the body. The drum should be parallel to the floor or tilted slightly away from the player.

Photo No. 2

There are three types of strokes which will need to be developed for all percussion playing. The first is the "full stroke"which begins in an up position, approximately 8" from the drum. The stick strikes the drum and rebounds to its original position. The stroke is relaxed and executed with the wrist, very similar to the bouncing of a basket ball. The arms will move, of course, but only because they are attached to the wrist. The motion is relaxed and fluid, and the stick rebounds freely. A "down stroke" begins in an up position and remains close to the drum head (about an inch) after striking. There is no rebound. The "up stroke" begins very close to the drum head (again, about an inch), strikes the drum and quickly moves to an up position. The importance of the "up stroke" and "down stroke" will become apparent when learning to properly execute rudiments involving flams and drags.

There are numerous ways to produce various dynamic levels at the snare drum. The height and velocity of the stokes will greatly effect the volume. That is, a stroke which is higher and faster will produce a relatively louder tone than one that is smaller and slower. For general playing, one should play near the center of the drum head, making certain both sticks are equidistant from the center. Moving closer to the edge of the drum will result in a diminishing dynamic and a change in tone color. Playing near the extreme edge produces a tone that is thin, ringing, and lacking in fundamental pitch. This area should only be used for extremely soft passages.

Snare Drum Maintenance and Tuning

Under active playing conditions, the batter head of a snare drum should be changed approximately once a year, and more often if it shows signs of unusual wear and tear. There are many fine manufacturers of plastic drum heads including Ludwig/Selmer, Remo, and Evans. A medium weight, coated head is recommended for general playing. When changing a head, one should use that opportunity to go through a number of maintenance procedures. Below is an outline:

1) Loosen any tension on the internal muffler, if one is present. Remove the tension rods and counterhoop from the batter head and clean them with a dry rag. (You will need a standard drum key.) Also, clean the inside of the drum.

2) Remove the old lubricant from the lugs and tension rods and replace with a dab of petroleum jelly.

3) Mount the new batter head and counterhoop and tension rods. Tighten all rods until they come in contact with the counterhoop.

4) Tighten each tension rod about 1/4 turn in the pattern diagramed below. Continue this process, diminishing the degree of turning until the correct tension is reached.

5) With the snares released, strike the batter head about two inches from each tension rod and listen carefully to the pitches. Find a "center" pitch. Bring down the higher pitches and bring up the lower pitches to match that center. Again, continue the tuning process as diagramed until the desired tension and tone is achieved.

6) With the snares released, check the pitch of the snare head. It should be slightly higher in pitch than the batter head (minor second to major third).

7) Use the "snare tension screw" to adjust the tension on the snares. If they are too loose, the drum will rattle when played loudly; if they are too tight, the drum will sound choked when played softly.

The sound of a good snare drum is often a matter of personal taste, but a few characteristics remain universal: The drum should be high in pitch, crisp and sharp. There should be a slight ring audible when standing directly at the drum, but not at a distance. The drum should be responsive. In other words, a drumstick should bounce freely to its original position when held loosely between the thumb and index finger. If the drum is properly tuned, an internal muffler should not be needed. If one finds it necessary to use the internal muffler, it should only touch the batter head enough to eliminate excess ring.

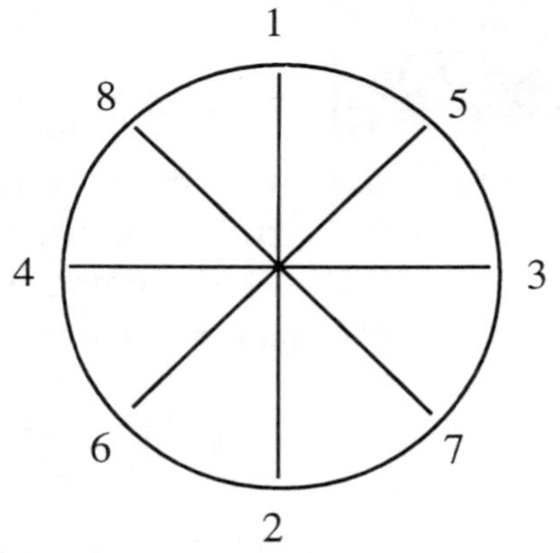

Tuning Pattern

Drum Sticks

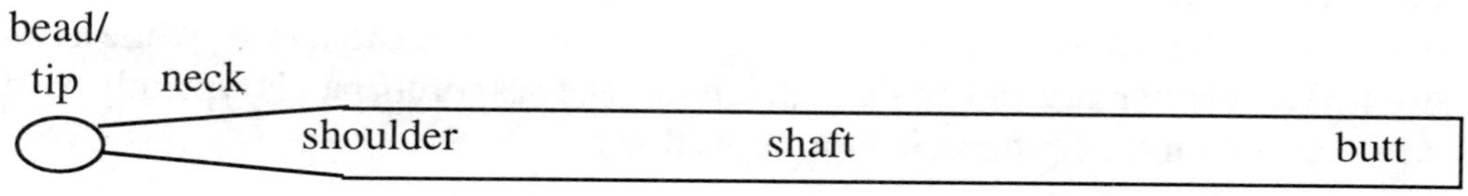

Excellent snare drum sticks are made from hardwoods such as hickory, maple, or oak. Some sticks have nylon tips which are used to produce a bright, articulate tone when played on cymbals. The bead size and shape will greatly effect the tone quality as will the weight of the stick. A smaller bead will usually produce a softer, more articulate tone while a larger bead produces a broad, dark tone. For many years, drum sticks were labeled with either an "A" (9/16" in diameter; suitable for orchestra/jazz playing), "B" (10/16" - "Band," general playing), or "S" (11/16" - "Street," - marching band). The number before the letter indicated bead size and type (i.e. 2B, 5A, 3S, etc.). In recent years manufactures have put less emphasis on this labeling system. A drum stick of medium weight and diameter (10/16") is recommended for general snare drum playing. Excellent sticks are manufactured by ProMark, Vic Firth, Regal, Ludwig, Yamaha, and Zildjian.

Drum Heads

Plastic heads are always recommended for use on a snare drum due to their relatively low cost and maintenance. Some professionals, however, prefer calf skin. There are numerous types of heads available commercially. Such a large variety can get a bit confusing for the amateur and professional alike, and one must be certain to know the exact brand, size, and style needed before purchasing a replacement. It is also very important to know whether one is purchasing a batter head or snare head. Snare heads are only available as "clear" and "x-thin." Batter heads, however, come in various weights (i.e. "thin," "medium," "heavy," "Ambassador™," Diplomat™," Emperor™," etc.) and in different styles (i.e. "coated," "opaque," "Silver dot™," "Pinstripe™," "Fiberskyn II™," "oil filled," "kevlar," etc.). For general snare drum playing, a medium weight coated batter head is recommended. For concert/drumset tom-toms, a dotted head, oil filled, or Pinstripe™ is recommended. With marching snare drums, a dotted head or kevlar is most popular. A heavy coated head, or Fiberskyn II™ is best suited for bass drums. Excellent drum heads are manufactured by Remo, Ludwig, and Evans.

Snares

There are three types of snares available: 1) wire - produces a bright tone; ideal for general playing; 2) gut - produces a dark, resonant tone; very popular with marching percussion; and 3) cable - the tone quality lies between that of gut and wire. This is preferred by many professionals. Cable is also very effective with marching percussion.

Bass Drum

The bass drum is the lowest voice of the percussion family. An instrument 16" X 36" (shell depth - 16", head diameter - 36") is ideal for high school, university and professional use, while a smaller drum, 16" X 32" is best suited for elementary and junior high school. The bass drum part is typically written on the same staff as the snare drum, on the first space with stems down.

The drum should be tuned low so as to produce a warm, resonant "boom." Tuning the drum too low, however, will result in a sound that is loose and flabby. The batter head may be tuned slightly lower than the opposite, resonating head.

Photo No. 3

There are three types of bass drum stands commercially available - the folding stand, tilting stand, and suspended/tilting stand. The tilting stands enable the player to employ a direct blow and allow the sound to be projected toward the floor enhancing its dark quality. The suspended stand is highly recommended due to the resulting increase in resonance.

Calf skin heads are highly recommended for their warmth and resonance. Fiberskyn™ heads (manufactured by REMO, Inc.) are an affordable and acceptable substitute for calf skin. Three mallets will suffice for most bass drum playing - a single heavy mallet with a dense core and a pair of lighter "rolling" mallets.

The player should be positioned behind the drum so he/she can see the instrument, the music and the conductor. There are three playing areas: 1) near the edge (produces a thin sound with little fundamental pitch and many high overtones); 2) dead center (dry, the least resonant playing area); and 3) slightly off center (the most resonant area with the most fundamental pitch. This area is used for the vast majority of playing situations.) The player should use a direct blow, never a glancing blow or up and down motion.

It may be necessary to muffle the drum in some manner if the sound is too resonant for a particular musical passage. Never fill the drum with muffling material nor put any muffling material on the head. While striking with the right hand, it is possible to rest the left hand on the batter head to help mute the sound. (See photo no. 3) One can also place the right knee against the batter head, with one's foot propped on a chair. Extremely short notes can be produced by placing the right knee against the batter head and the left hand against the resonating head. Rolling on the drum isdone with a pair of identical mallets. Never use a single mallet (or doubled-headed mallet) to produce a roll. The roll is made by single strokes. The louder the dynamic, the faster the roll.

Crash Cymbals

There are numerous sizes, weights, and types of crash cymbals commercially available. "Thin," or "French" cymbals are characterized by a light texture, bright tone, fast response and quick decay. "Medium" weight cymbals (often called "symphonic" or "Viennese") are for general purpose playing. "Heavy" cymbals ("Wagnerian," "Germanic") are suitable for single fortissimo crashes. They are generally darker in tone color and a bit slower in response and decay. The qualities inherent in a fine pair of cymbals are: 1) response - the cymbals should reach maximum vibration quickly and easily; 2) resonance - the cymbals should possess a thick palate and full range of overtones without any fundamental pitch; and 3) a relatively long duration of vibration. Cymbals manufactured by Zildjian, Sabian, or Paiste are of the highest professional quality.

A pair of 18" medium weight cymbals are highly recommended as the principal cymbals for most symphonic ensembles. Leather straps should be used to hold the cymbals. (See the diagram below for the proper tying of a cymbal knot.) Never use wooden handles. Avoid using lambs wool or leather pads with the cymbals as they have a tendency to inhibit the vibrations. The leather straps are held **without** placing one's hands through them. (Drum corps style cymbal playing often requires putting one's hands through the straps, however.) Grasp the strap between the thumb and index finger close to the bell. Wrap the other fingers securely around the strap so as to make a fist. Pull the fist down against the bell. The thumb may rest on the bell of the cymbal to help support it. The cymbal player should stand erect with one foot in front of the other to help maintain balance at all times. The cymbals are held chest high.

The most effective cymbal crash results when both plates are in motion, striking each other with a glancing blow. The plates are held on an angle to one another and strike each other slightly off center (about 1/2" - 1"). As one cymbal moves down and out, the other moves up and out. (See photo no. 5) The player may end up with both plates facing the audience or hanging at his side.

Different dynamic levels will require slight variations to the above mentioned crash technique. Very soft crashes can be played with the plates parallel to one another, in a vertical position, and about 1" - 2" apart. The plates remain parallel to each other after the crash. (See photo no. 4) For a medium loud crash, the plates are held farther apart and at a slight angle. (See photo no. 5) After the crash the arms will "follow through" and separate. For a very loud crash, both the distance and angle of the plates are increased. (See photo no. 6) For a rapid sequence of crashes, one can hold the left cymbal stationary and crash the right against it with a glancing blow.

To dampen the cymbals simply touch the edges of each plate against the upper body. Doing this very rapidly after a crash is often referred to as "choking" the cymbals.

Tying the cymbal knot **:**

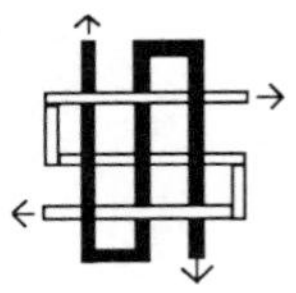

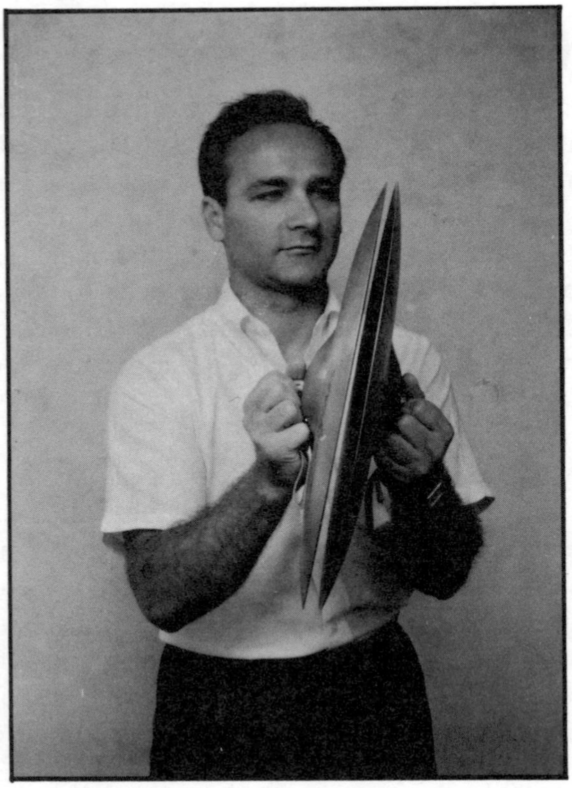

Photo No. 4

Photo No. 5

Photo No. 6

Triangle

The characteristic sound of the triangle is one that is long, sustained, and highly complex, with many shimmering overtones. An instrument of either 6" or 8" is suitable for general playing. One should have a number of beaters of various weights available to produce different dynamics and tone colors. The triangle should be suspended with nylon fishing line or thin gut from a standard triangle clip. Never use string, wire, or a finger to suspend the triangle.

To hold the triangle, one should extend his/her left hand at eye level, as if to hold a drink. The triangle clip rests on the thumb and first finger while the triangle hangs below. Hold the triangle beater with the thumb and first two fingers of the right hand.

Strike the instrument on the bottom bar with a full stroke and lift the beater away. It is important to hold the instrument at eye level so one can watch the instrument, the music, and the conductor simultaneously. Do not overplay the triangle: Doing so will result in an unpleasant "clang" and will also cause the instrument to turn.

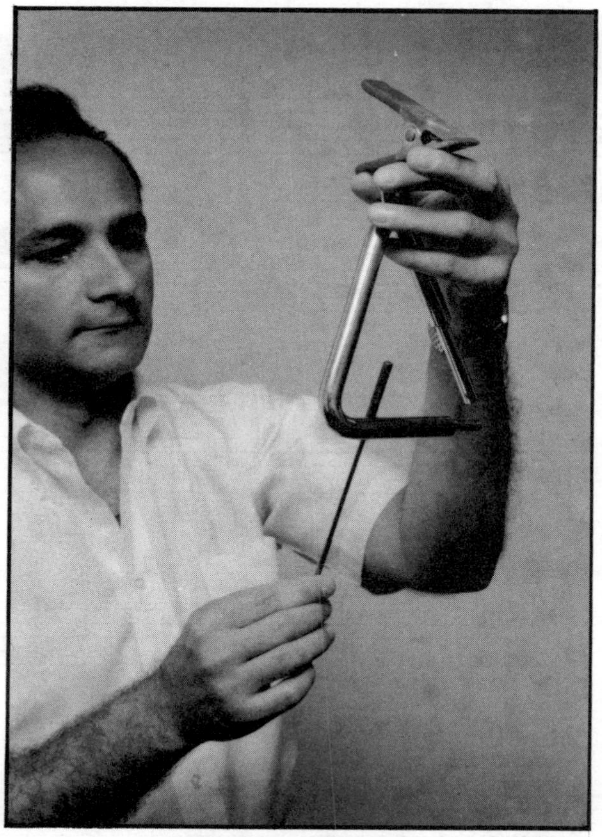

To dampen the triangle, simply close the fingers of the left hand around the clip and triangle. A roll on the instrument is produced by rapid up and down strokes in a **closed** corner. (Use rapid side to side strokes in the top corner.)

Dynamic changes may be obtained by using beaters of different weights, and strokes of varying lengths and velocities. Smaller, slower strokes will produce a softer tone while larger, faster strokes will produce a louder tone.

LESSON 1

Sticking combinations - Practice this lesson daily. Start slowly and gradually increase the tempo over time. Repeat each line many times.

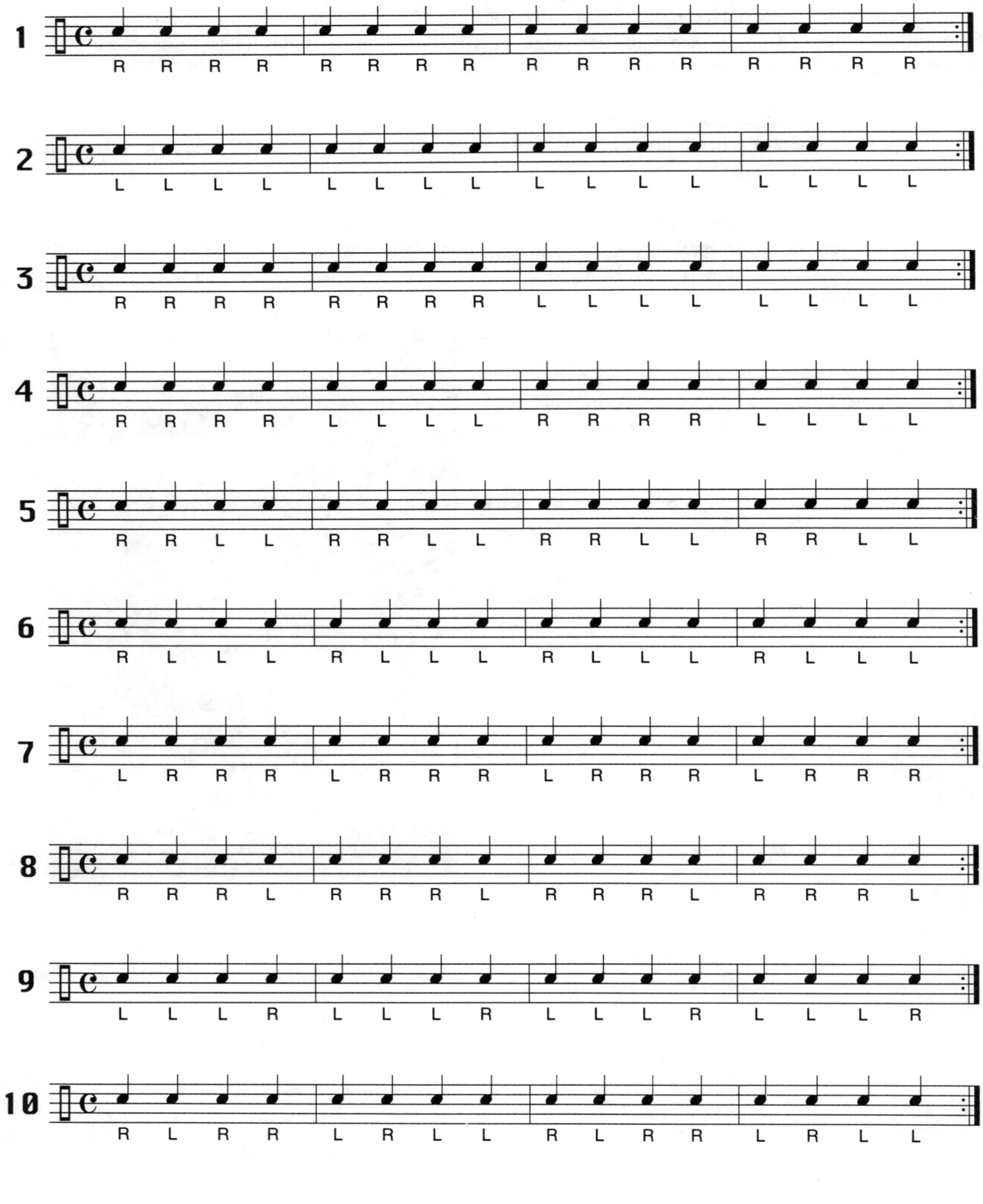

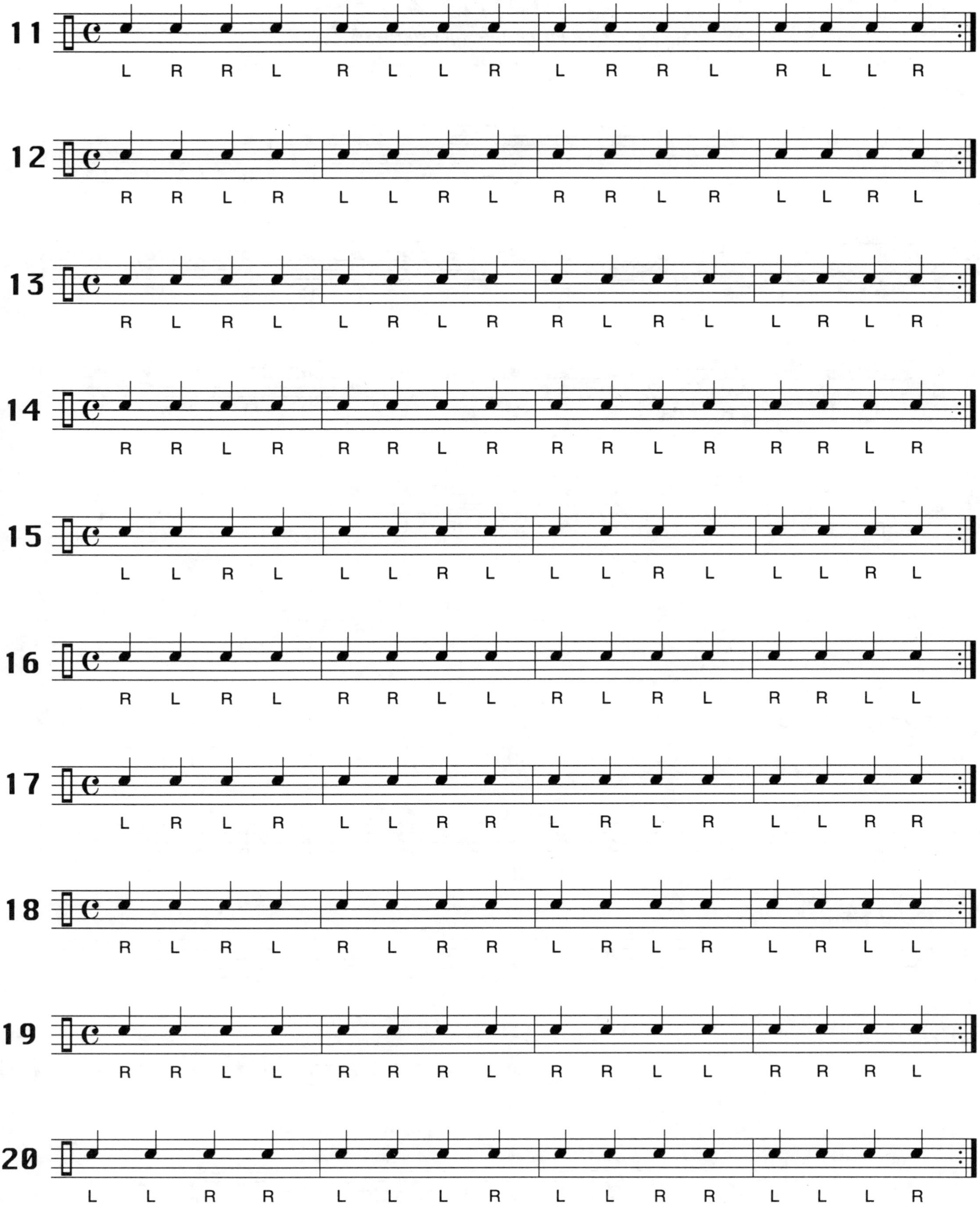
11
L R R L R L L R L R R L R L L R
12
R R L R L L R L R R L R L L R L
13
R L R L L R L R R L R L L R L R
14
R R L R R R L R R R L R R R L R
15
L L R L L L R L L L R L L L R L
16
R L R L R R L L R L R L R R L L
17
L R L R L L R R L R L R L L R R
18
R L R L R L R R L R L R L R L L
19
R R L L R R R L R R L L R R R L
20
L L R R L L L R L L R R L L L R

LESSON 2

Reading quarter notes/quarter rests

1

2

3
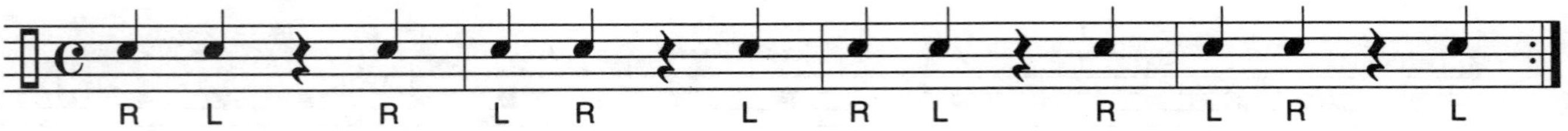

4

5

6

7

8

9

10

LESSON 3

Reading eighth notes/eighth rests

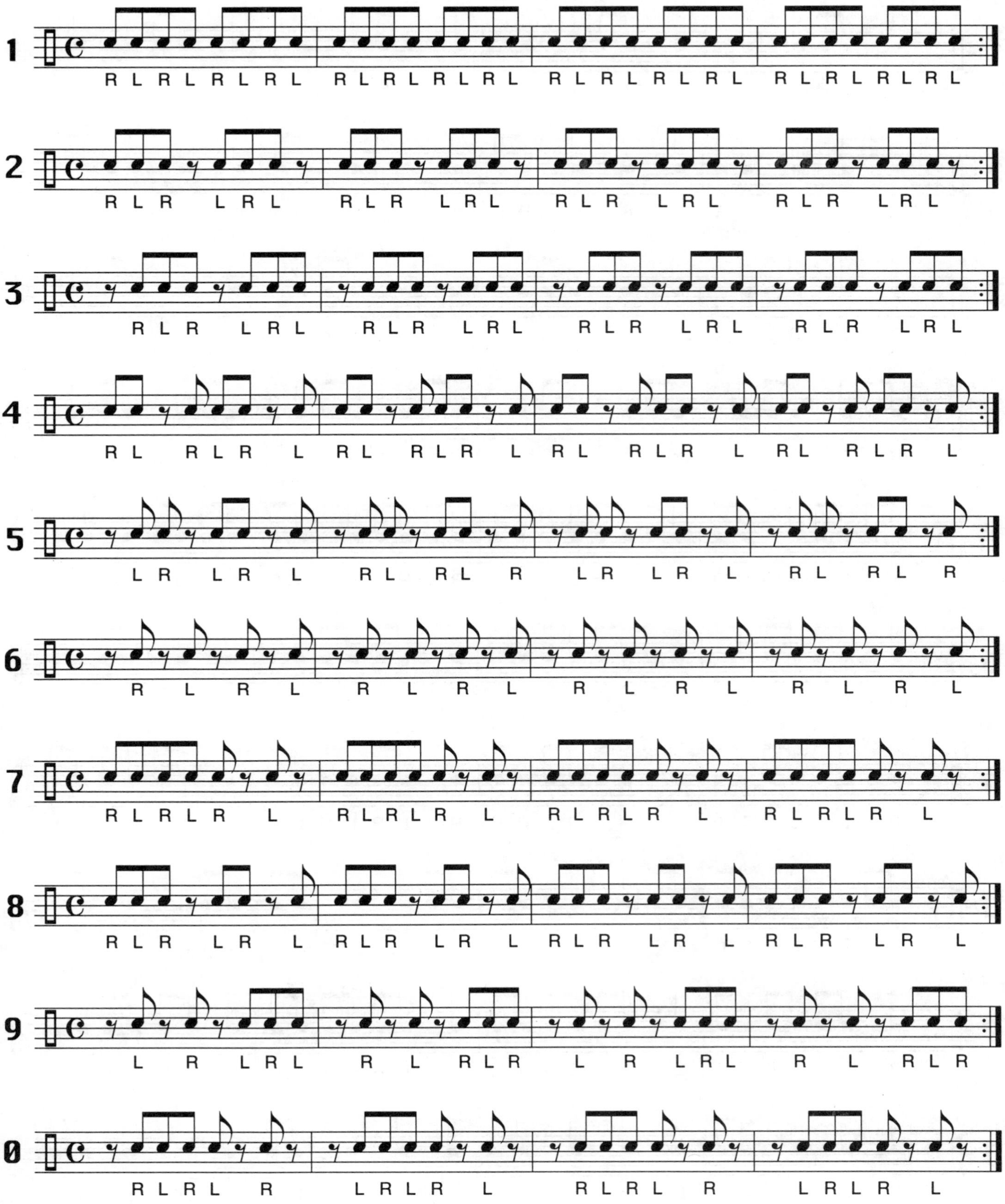

LESSON 4

Quarter notes and eighth notes

1

2

3

4

5

6

7

8

9

10

LESSON 5

quarter notes, eighth notes, quarter rests

ETUDE NO. 1

Terms and Symbols for Etudes 1-3:

f = forte - loud

p = piano - soft

Moderato = moderately fast

First and Second Endings = on repeat, skip first ending and play the second ending

< = crescendo - gradually get louder

> = decrescendo - gradually get softer

mf = mezzo forte - moderately loud

mp = mezzo piano - moderately soft

ff = fortissimo - very loud

pp = pianissimo - very soft

Allegro = fast

molto = much

ritard = gradually slow down

ETUDE NO. 2

ETUDE NO. 3

LESSON 6

Studies in 2/4

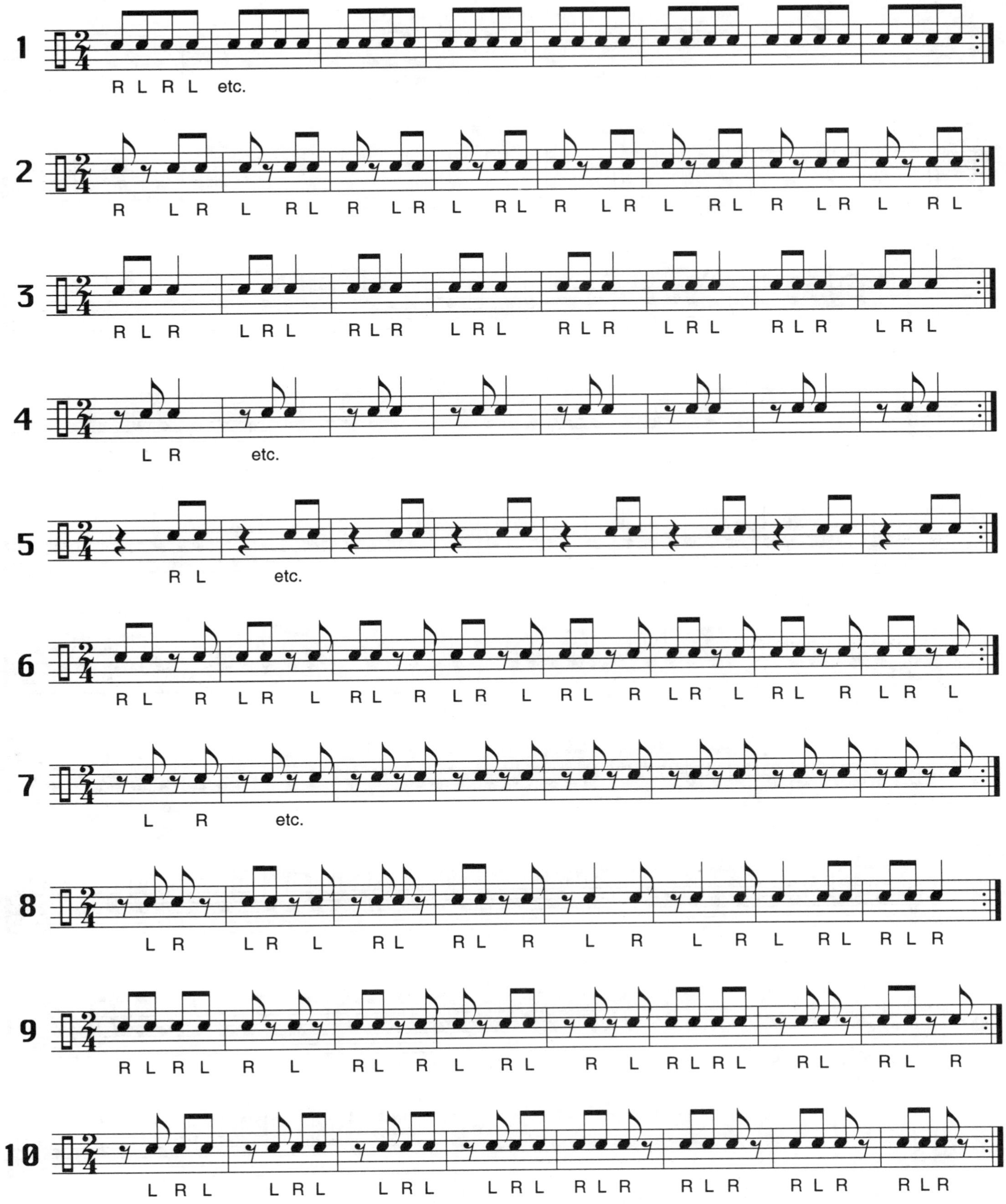

LESSON 7

Studies in 3/4

1

2

3

4

5

6

7

8

9

10

LESSON 8

Paradiddles

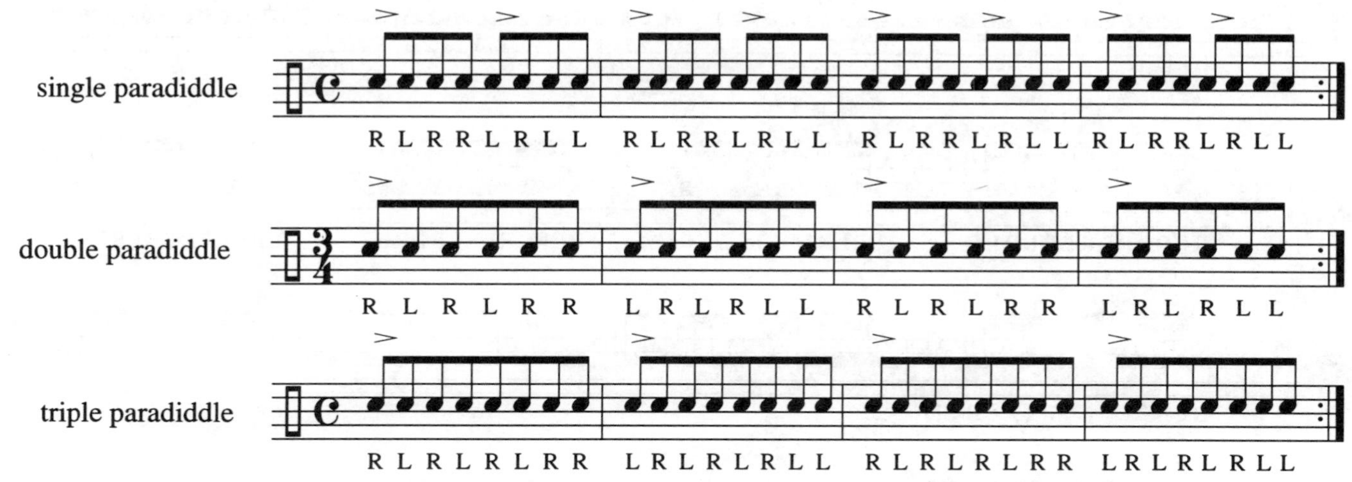
single paradiddle
R L R R L R L L R L R R L R L L R L R R L R L L R L R R L R L L
double paradiddle
R L R L R R L R L R L L R L R L R R L R L R L L
triple paradiddle
R L R L R L R R L R L R L R L L R L R L R L R R L R L R L R L L

Paradiddle Etude

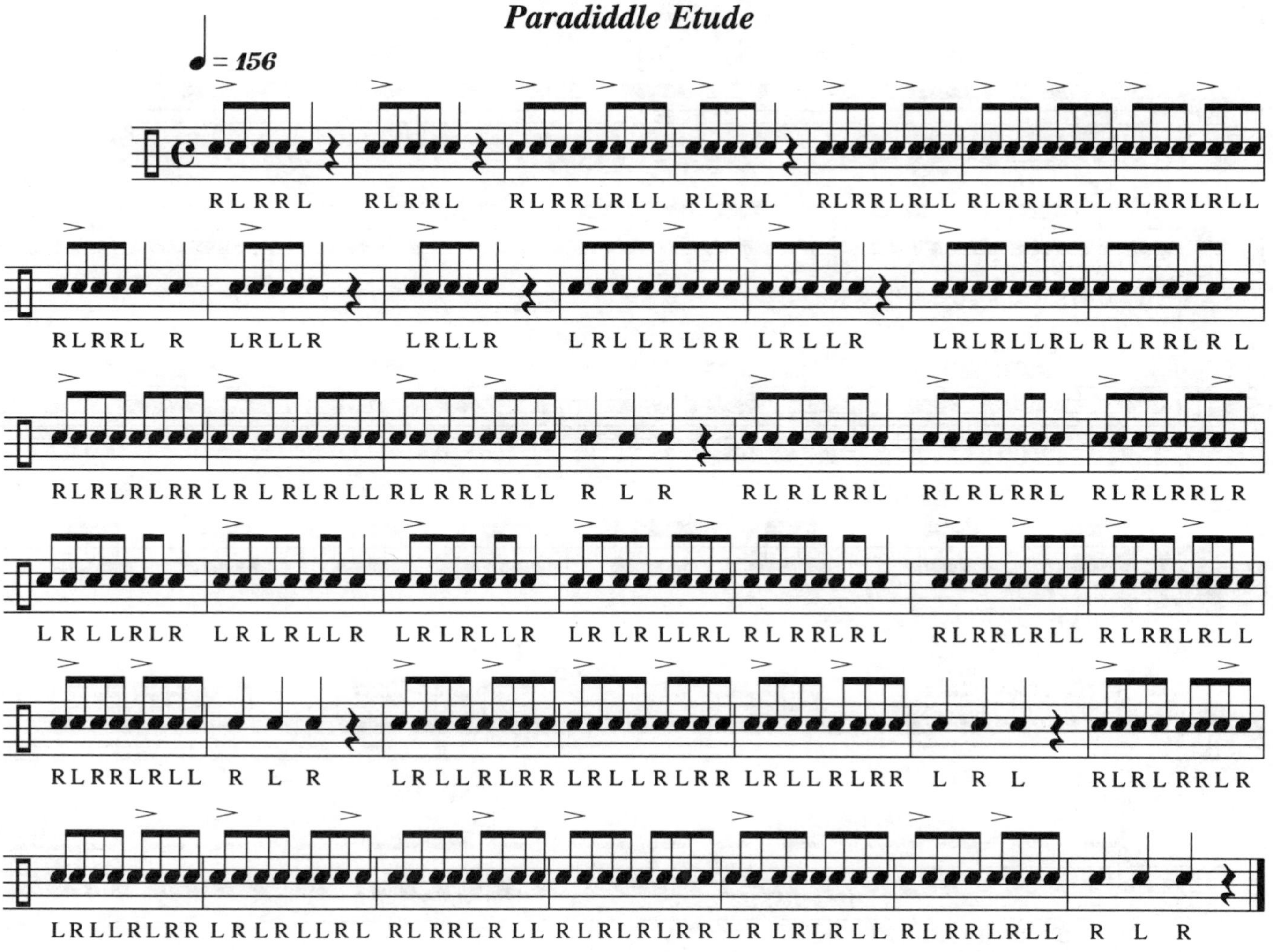
= 156
RLRRL RLRRL RLRRLRLL RLRRL RLRRLRLL RLRRLRLL RLRRLRLL
RLRRL R LRLLR LRLLR LRLLRLRR LRLLR LRLRLLRL RLRRLRL
RLRLRLRR LRLRLRLL RLRRLRLL R L R RLRLRRL RLRLRRL RLRLRRLR
LRLLRLR LRLRLLR LRLRLLR LRLRLLRL RLRRLRL RLRRLRLL RLRRLRLL
RLRRLRLL R L R LRLLRLRR LRLLRLRR LRLLRLRR L R L RLRLRRLR
LRLLRLRR LRLRLLRL RLRRLRLL RLRLRLRR LRLRLRLL RLRRLRLL R L R

LESSON 9

Sixteenth note study

1

RLRL etc.

2

RLRLRLRLRLRLR   LRLRLRLRLRLRL   RLRLRLRLRLRLR   LRLRLRLRLRLRL

3

RLRLR L RLRLR L etc.

4

R L R L RLRLR L etc.

5

R L RLRLR   L R LRLRL   R L RLRLR   L R LRLRL

6

R L R L R L R L R L R L R

7

R LRLRL R L etc.

8

RLRLR RLRLR etc.

9

R LRLRLRLRLRL etc.

10

R L R L R LRLRL etc.

LESSON 10

Sixteenth notes continued

1

R L R L R L R L R L R L etc.

2

RL R L R L RL R L R L etc.

3

R L RLR L R LRL etc.

4

RLR L R LRL R L etc.

5

RLRLRLR LRLRLRL etc.

6

R LRL R LRL R L RLR L RLR L R LRL R LRL R L RLR L RLR L

7

R L R L R LRLRL etc.

8

R LRLRLRLRLRL etc.

9

RLR LRLRL RLR LRL RLRLR LRL RLR LRLRL RLR LRL RLRLR LRL

10

RLRLR L R LRLRL etc.

LESSON 11

Sixteenth notes/Sixteenth rests

1 

RLR L RLR L etc.

2 

R LR LRLRL RL etc.

3 

RLRLR LRLRL etc.

4 

RLRLRL RLRLRL etc.

5 

RLR LRL etc.

6 

RL etc.

7 

RL etc.

8 

R LRLRLRL R L RLRLRLR L R LRLRLRL R L RLRLRLR L

9 

RLRLRL etc.

10 

R LR L RLR L RL R LRL R LR L RLR L RL R LRL

ETUDE NO. 4

New Terms and Symbols:

D.S. al Fine = *Dal Segno al Fine* - go back to the sign, play to the fine

× = rim shot - lay one stick against head and rim, strike with other stick

ETUDE NO. 5

Presto = very fast

> = accent - slightly louder

D.C. al Coda = Da Capo al Coda - Go back to beginning and play to Coda sign, then skip to the Coda and play to end of piece.

ETUDE NO. 6

Andante = moderately fast

LESSON 12

Sixteenth note rests

1
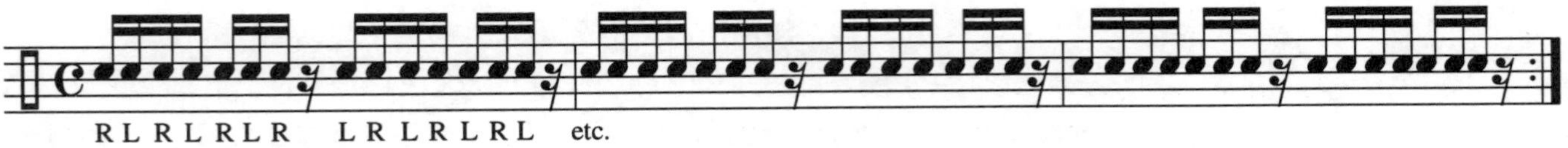

2

3

4

5

6

7

8

9

10

LESSON 13

Sixteenth rests continued

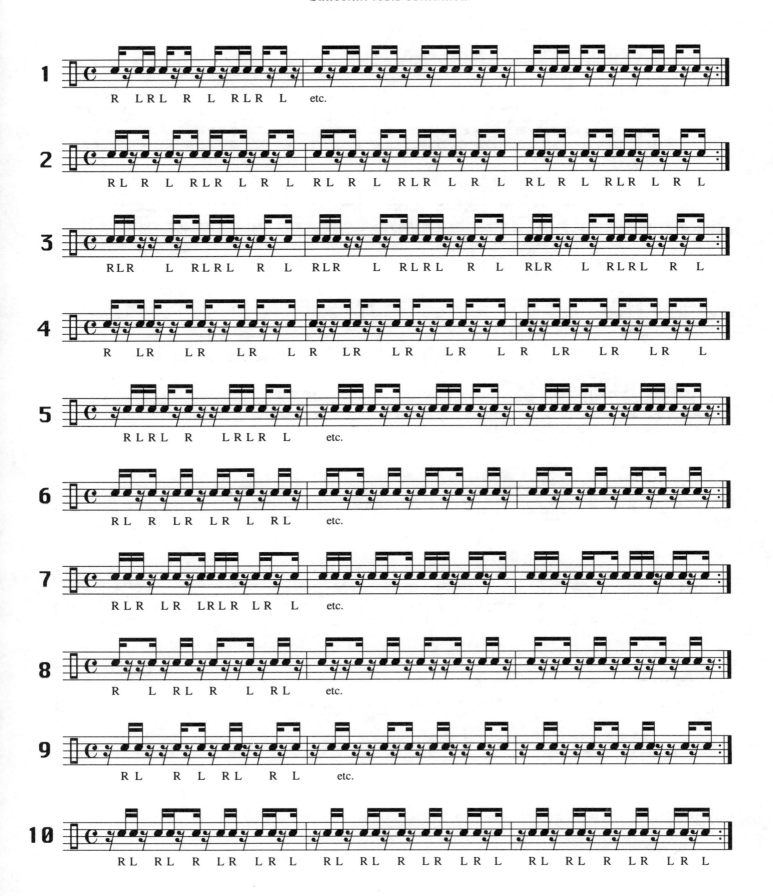

1

2

3

4

5

6

7

8

9

10

ETUDE NO. 7

LESSON 14

Dotted notes

1 

2 

3 

4 

5 

6 

7 

8 

9 

10 

LESSON 15

Tied notes

LESSON 16

Studies in 6/8

1 

2 

3 

4 

5 

6 

7 

8 

9 

10 

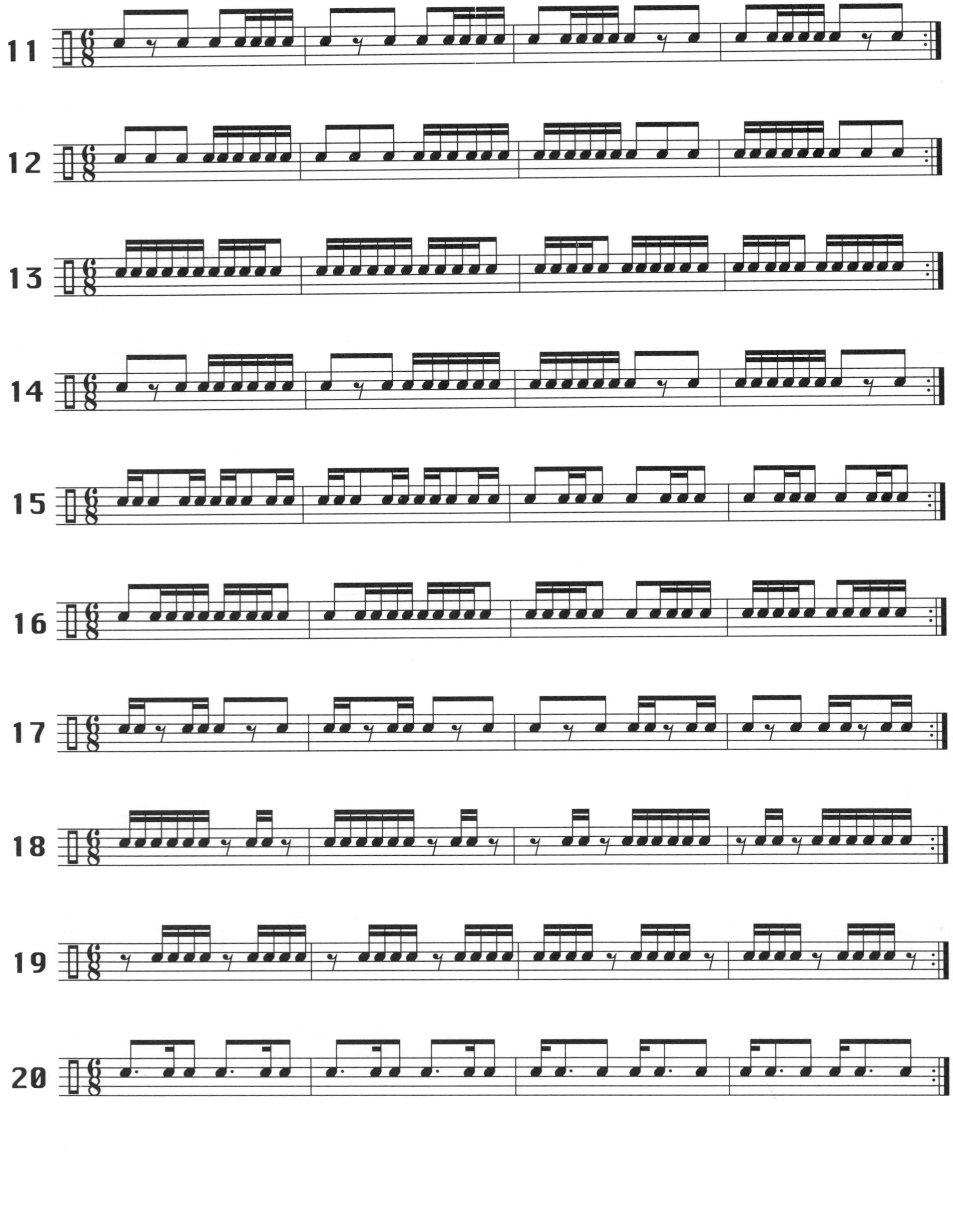
11
12
13
14
15
16
17
18
19
20

LESSON 17

Studies in ₵

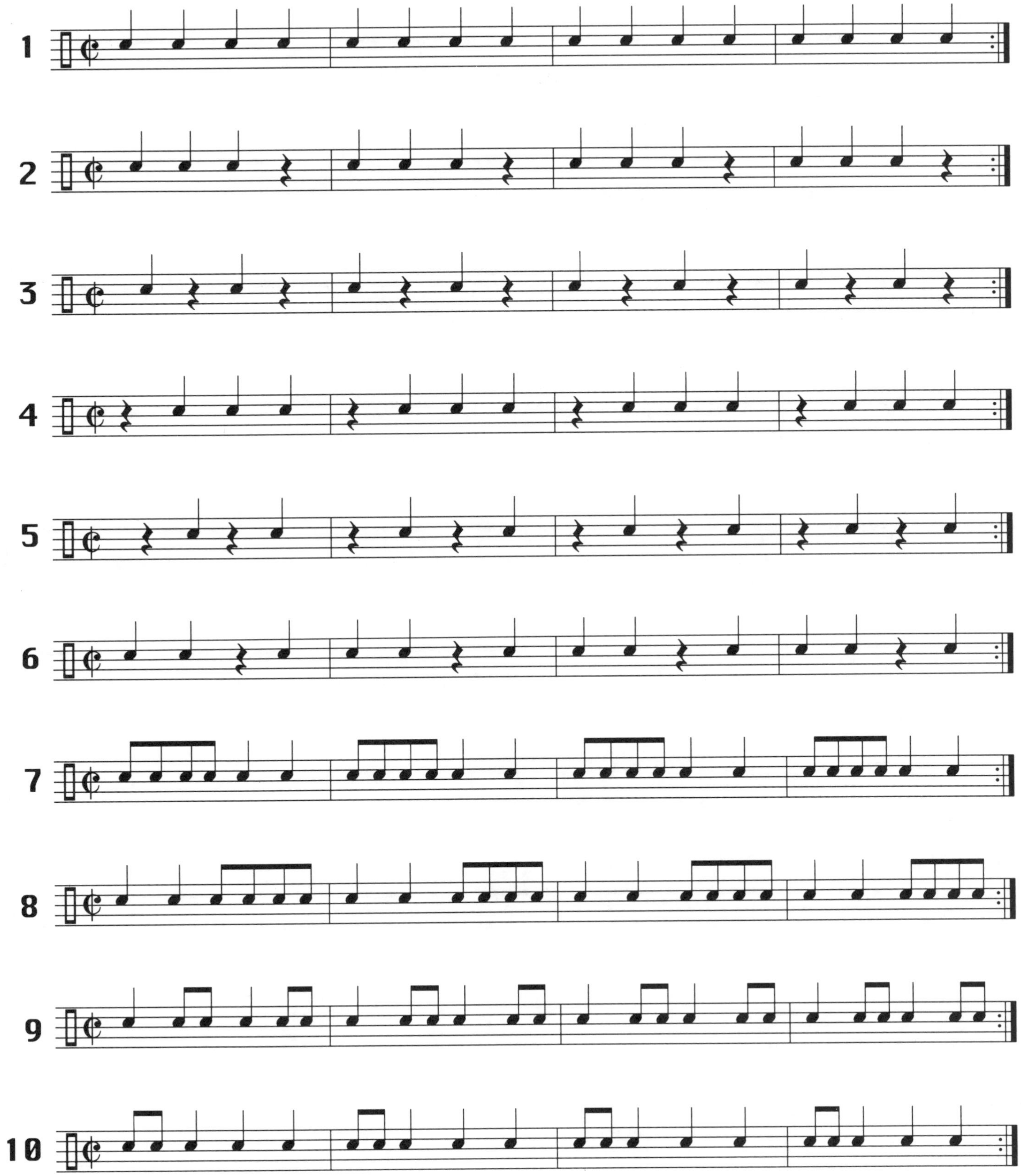

11

12

13

14

15

16

17

18

19

20

LESSON 18

Triplets

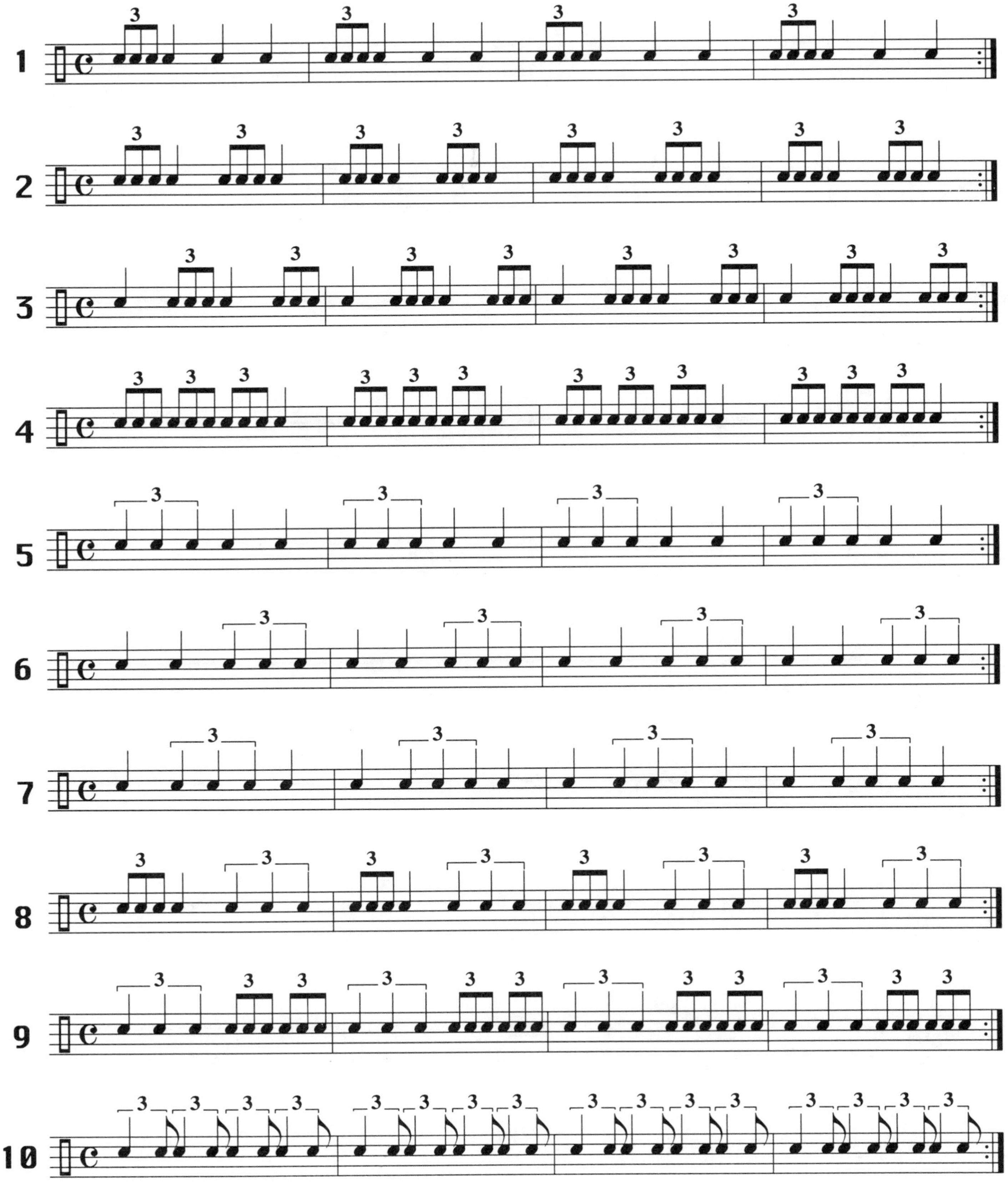

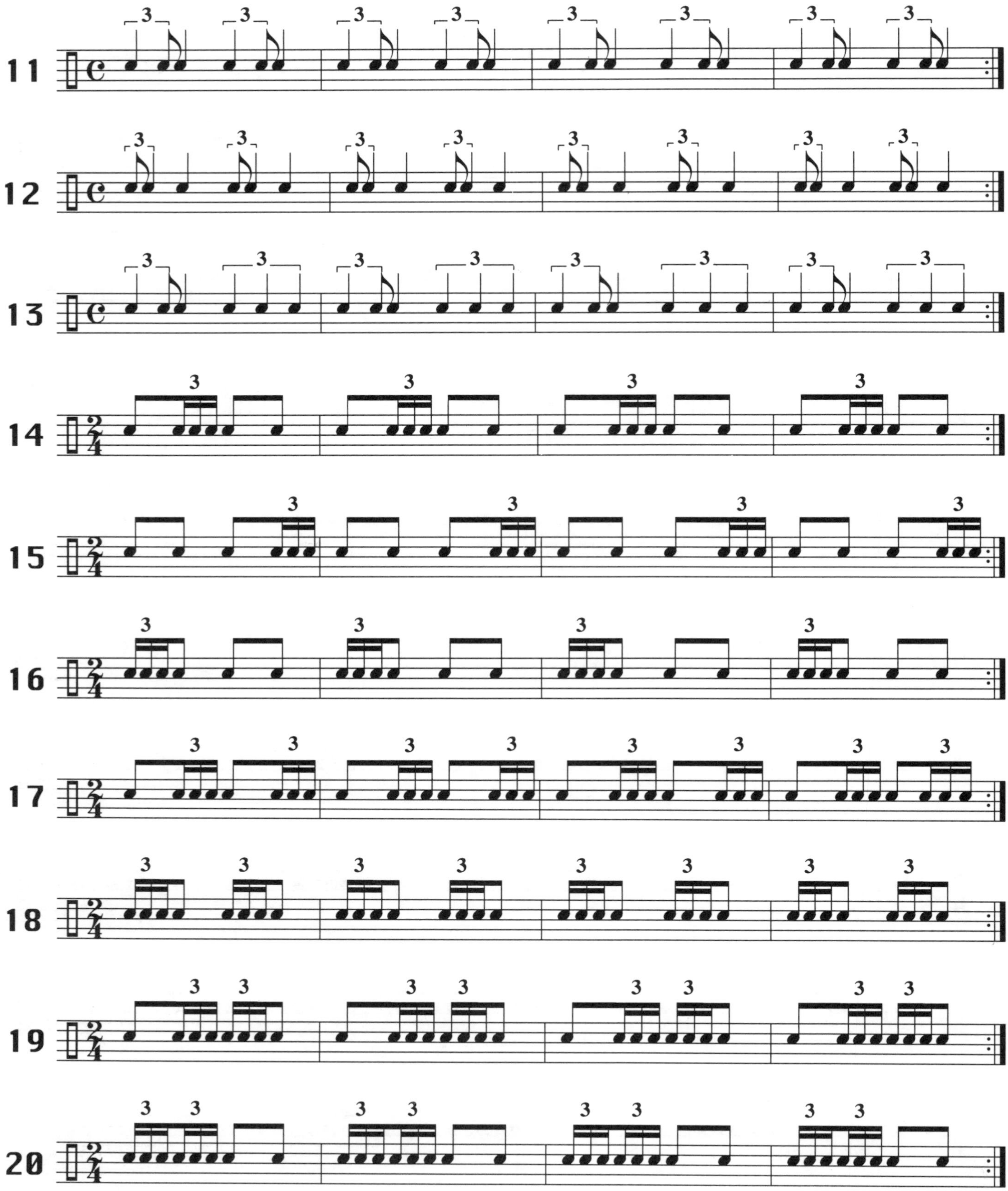
11
12
13
14
15
16
17
18
19
20

ETUDE NO. 8

ETUDE NO. 9

LESSON 19

flams

A flam consists of two alternating strokes - a grace note quickly followed by a principal note. To execute the flam, hold one stick approximately 1/2" - 1" from the drum head and the other stick in a normal up position. (See photo) The stick close to the head plays an upstroke while the stick held in the up position plays a down stroke. The hands finish in the reverse position from where they started, in preparation for the next flam. One must be certain that the sound produced is similar to the word "flam." The most common errors with beginning players is a flam that is either too open or too closed (referred to as "flat"). The player must also be certain to execute the flam with a straight up and down motion, as opposed to a side to side or in and out motion. The grace note will sound much softer than the principal note due to the nature of its positioning. Flams should be practiced very slowly and methodically at first.

1

2

3

4

5

6
lR L R rL R L etc.
7
lR rL lR L R rL lR rL R L lR rL lR L R rL lR rL R L
8
lR rL lR L R rL lR rL R L lR rL lR L R rL lR rL R L
9
lR LRL RrL RLR L etc.
10
lRLRrLRLlRLRrLRL etc.
11
lRLRrL RLlRLRrL RL etc.
12
lRLRLR L R LlR rLRLRL R L RrL lRLRLR L R LlR rLRLRL R L RrL
13
lRLRLR LlR L R rLRLRL RrL R L lRLRLR LlR L R rLRLRL RrL R L
14
lRLRLR L R LlRLRL etc.

LESSON 20

Flam taps

1

2

3

4

5

6

7

8

9

10

ETUDE NO. 10

LESSON 21

Studies in Syncopation

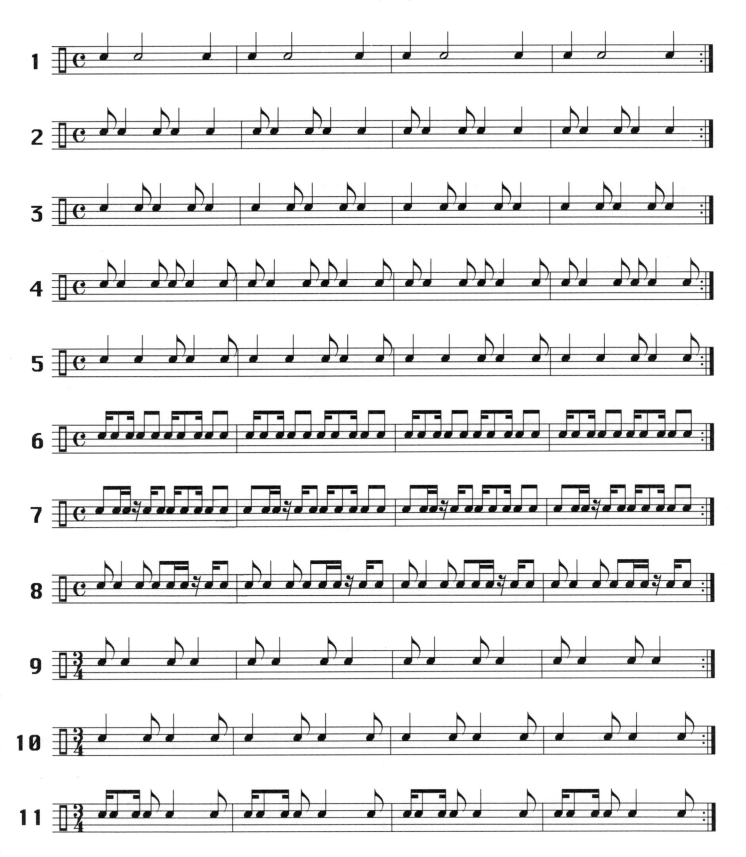

1 

2 

3 

4 

5 

6 

7 

8 

9 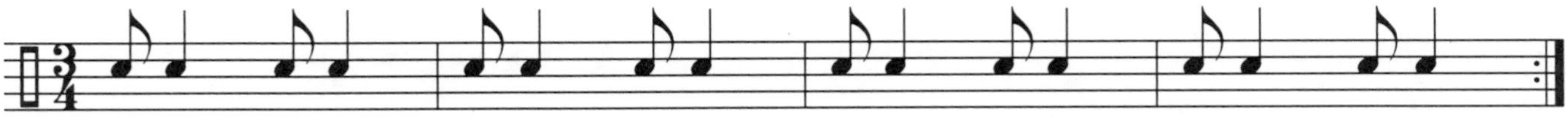

10 

11 

LESSON 22

Additional flam rudiments

Flam Accent

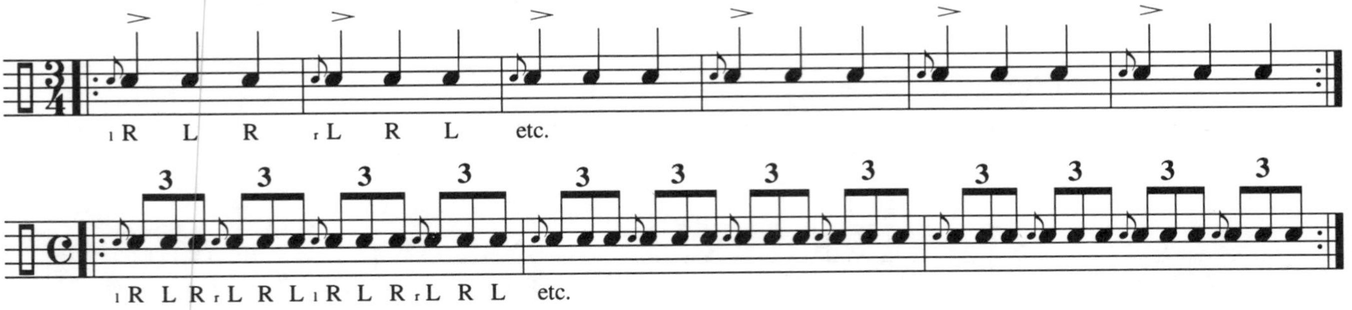

Flamacue

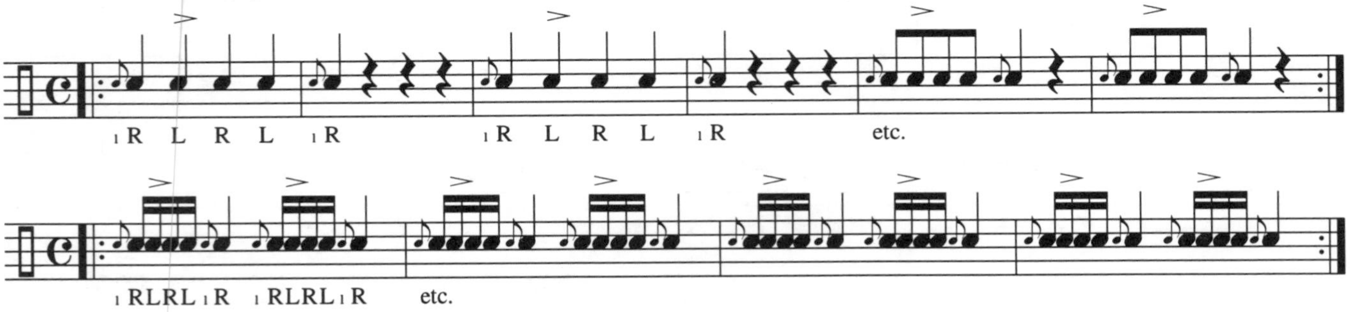

Flam Paradiddle

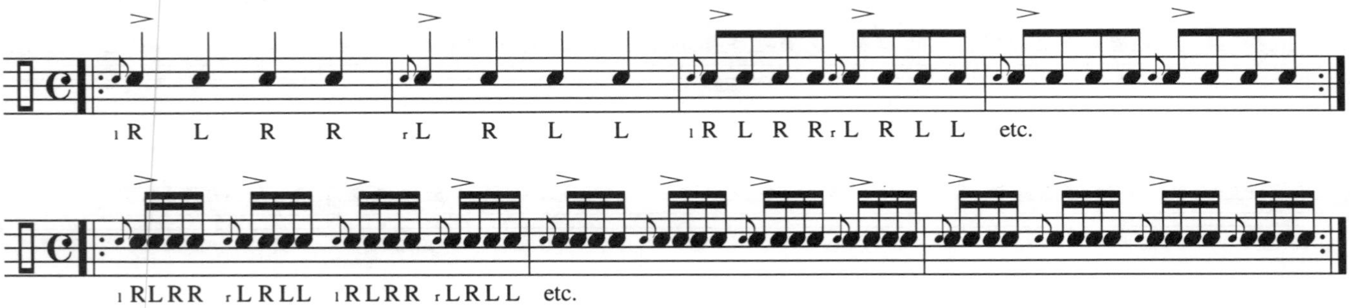

Flam Paradiddle-diddle

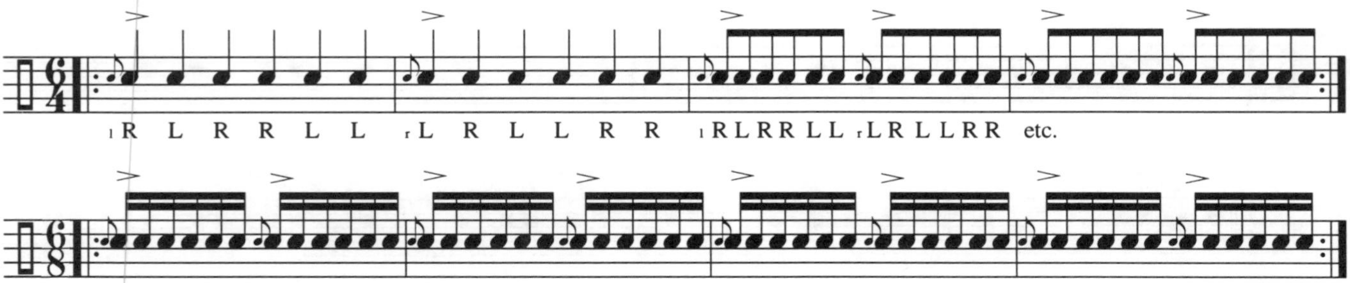

ETUDE NO. 11

ETUDE NO. 12

= 60
(flam tap)
(flam accent)
f
fine
f–p
ff
pp
ff
pp
f
(flam paradiddle-diddle)
D.C. al Fine
p

LESSON 23

5-stroke roll

1

RLR LRL RLR LRL RRLLR LLRRL RRLLR LLRRL R R L L R R L L

2

R LRL RLR LRL RL R LLRR LRRLL R LLRR LRRLL R L L R R L L R

3

RLR LRL R LRL RL RRLLR LLRRL R LLRR L RRLL R R L L R L L R

4

R L L R L R R L R L L R L R R L R L L R L R R L R L L R L R R L

5

R R L R L L R L R R L R L L R L R R L R L L R L R R L R L L R L

6

RLRLR R LRLRL L RLRLR R LRLRL L RLRLR R LRLRL L RLRLR R LRLRL L

7

RLRLR L LRLRL R RLRLR L LRLRL R RLRLR L LRLRL R RLRLR L LRLRL

8

R R L L RLRLR R L L R R LRLRL L R R L L RLRLR R L L R R LRLRL L

9

R L L R RLRLR L L R R L LRLRL R R L L R RLRL R L L R R L LRLRL

10

R RLR L R RLR L R RLR L R RLR L R RLR L R RLR L R RLR L R RLR L

ETUDE NO. 13

LESSON 24

Nine-stroke roll

1

2
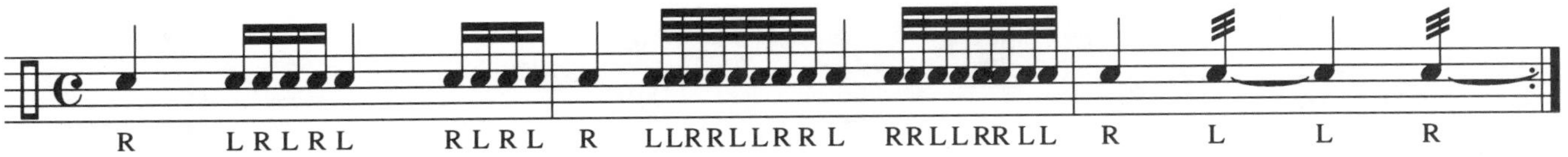

3

4

5

6

7

8

9

10

ETUDE NO. 14

LESSON 25

Thirteen-stroke roll

Seventeen-stroke roll

ETUDE NO. 15

LESSON 26

Seven-stroke roll

The seven-stroke roll can be performed in two manners. The first is a more rudimental approach, as a dotted eighth note. The second is a more concert approach, as a sixteenth-note triplet. Both should be studied and implemented in their respective styles.

As a dotted eighth note

1 

2 

3 

4 

As a sixteenth-note triplet

1 

2 

3 

4 

5 

ETUDE NO. 16

ETUDE NO. 17

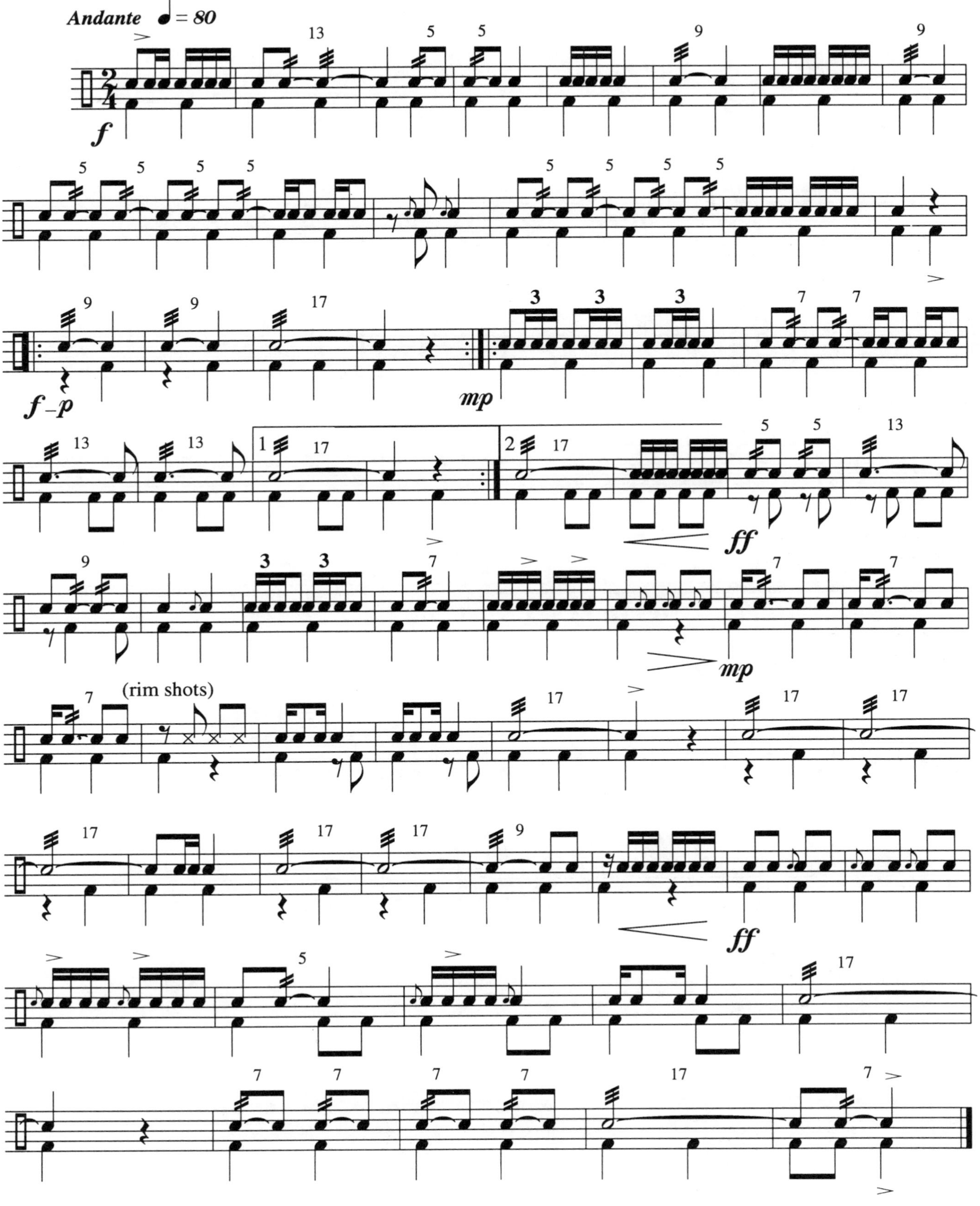

ETUDE NO. 18

LESSON 27

Eleven-stroke roll

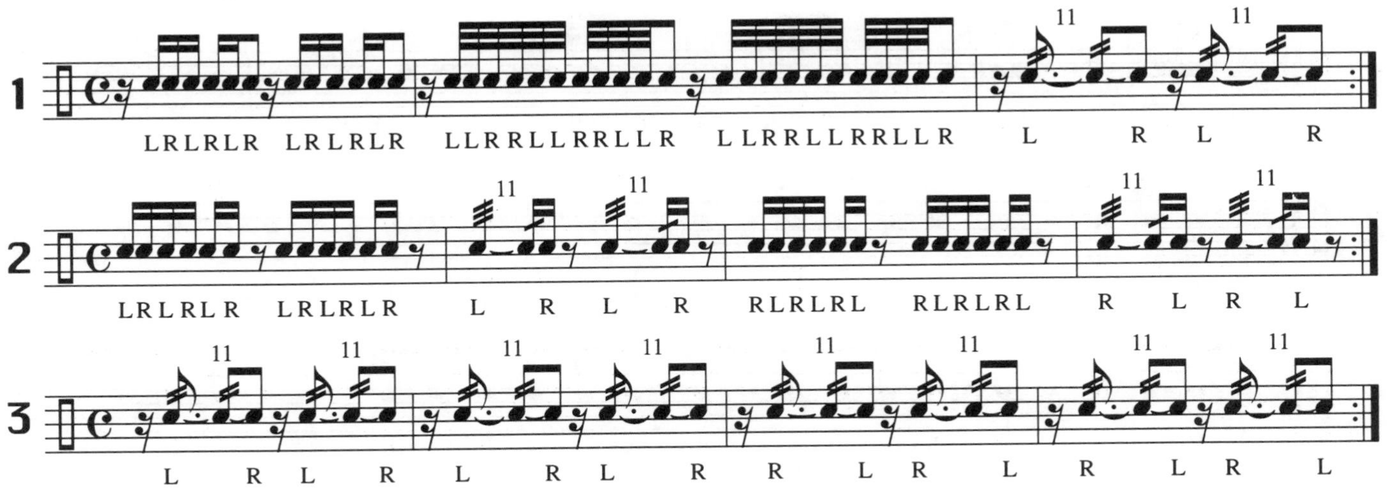

Fifteen-stroke roll

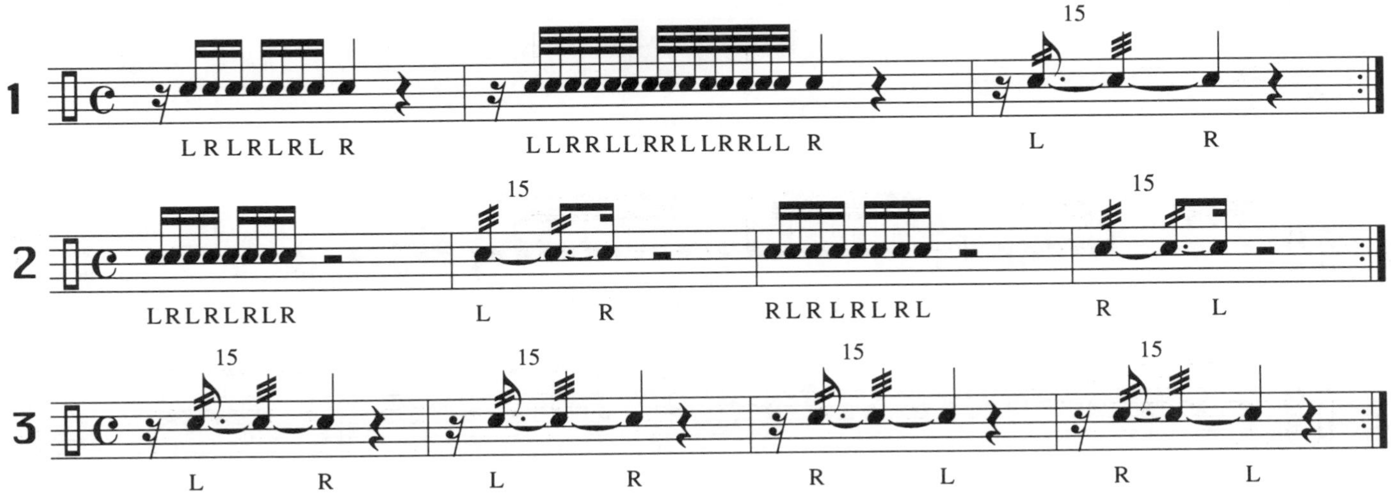

LESSON 28

Rolls in 6/8 (six beats per bar)

Five-stroke roll

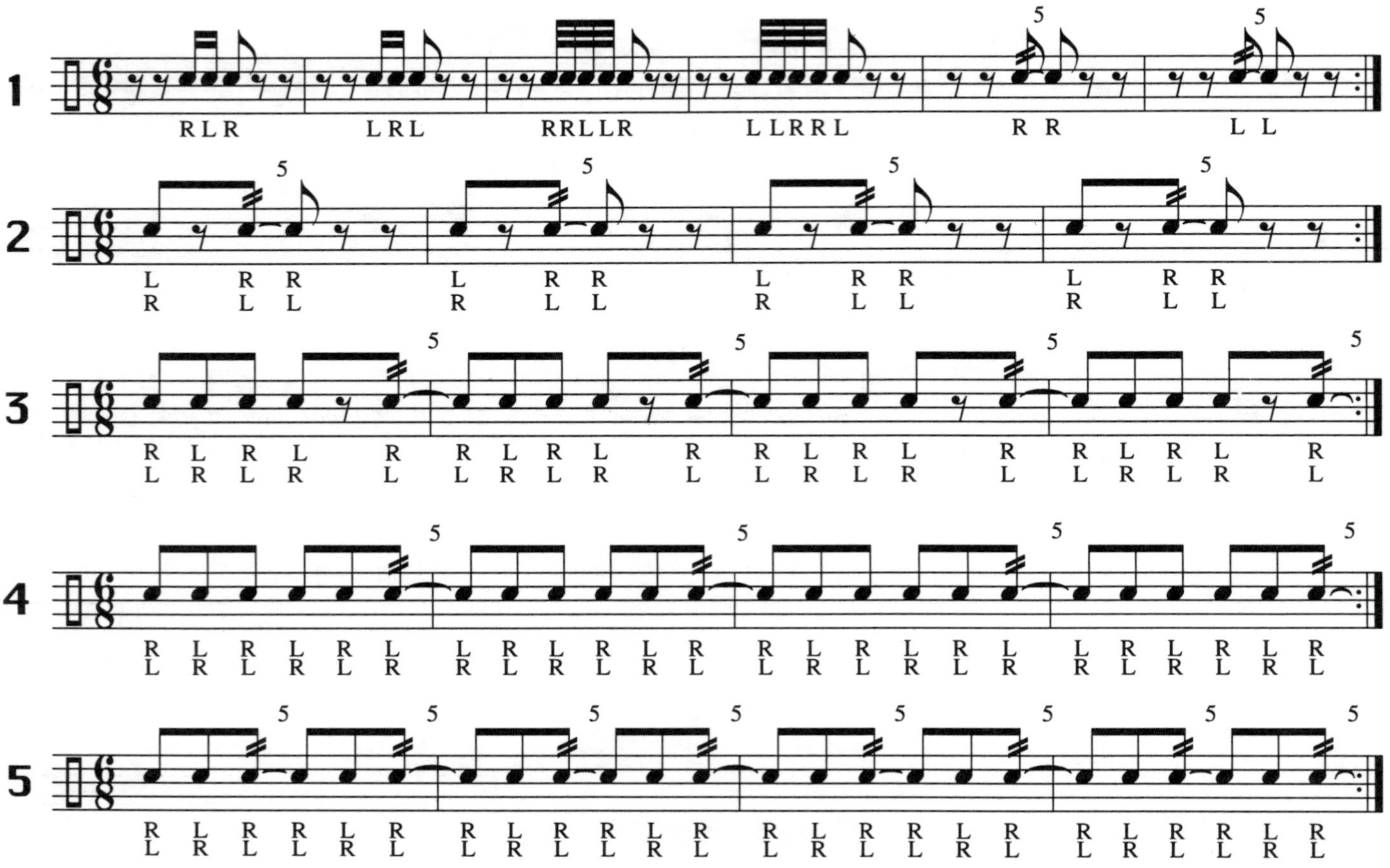

Nine-stroke roll

Thirteen-stroke roll

ETUDE NO. 19

LESSON 29

Rolls in 6/8 (2 beats per bar)

Five-stroke roll

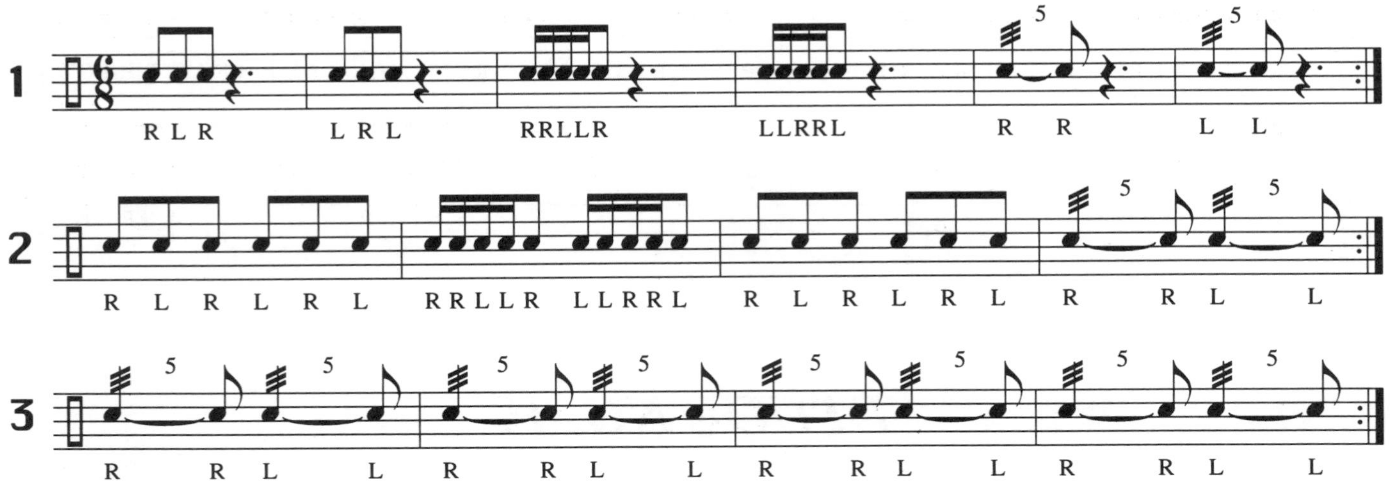

Seven-stroke roll

Thirteen-stroke roll

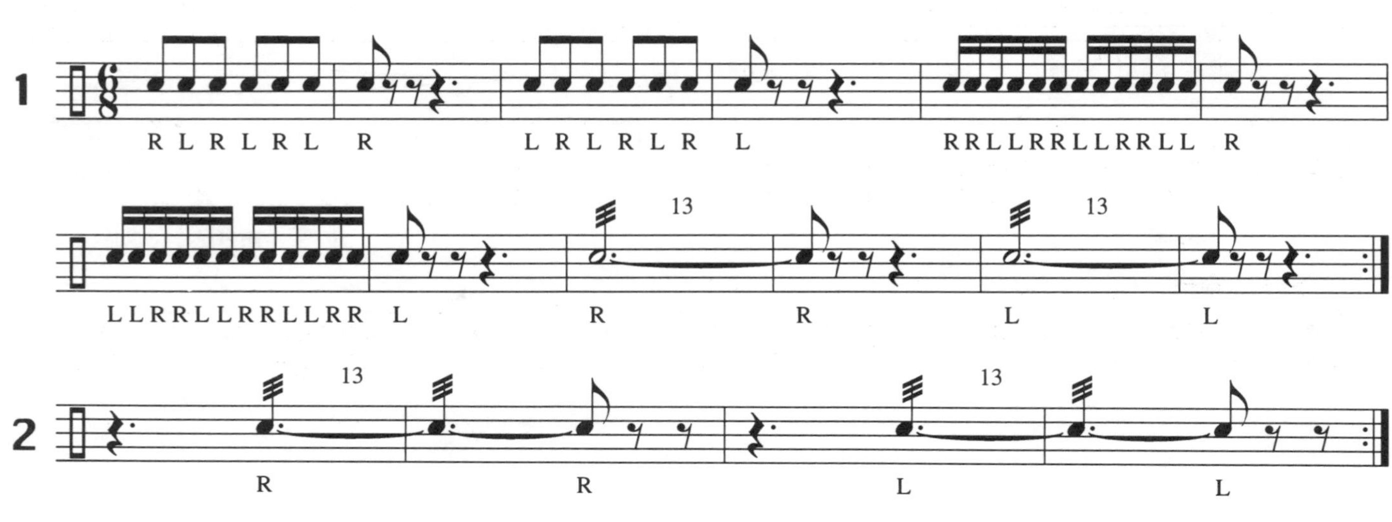

ETUDE NO. 20

LESSON 30

The Drag

(grace notes are played softer than principal notes)

The Four-Stroke Ruff

(grace notes are played softer than principal notes)

LESSON 31

Ratamacues

Single Ratamacues

1

2

3

Double Ratamacues

1

2

3

Triple Ratamacues

1

2

ETUDE NO. 21

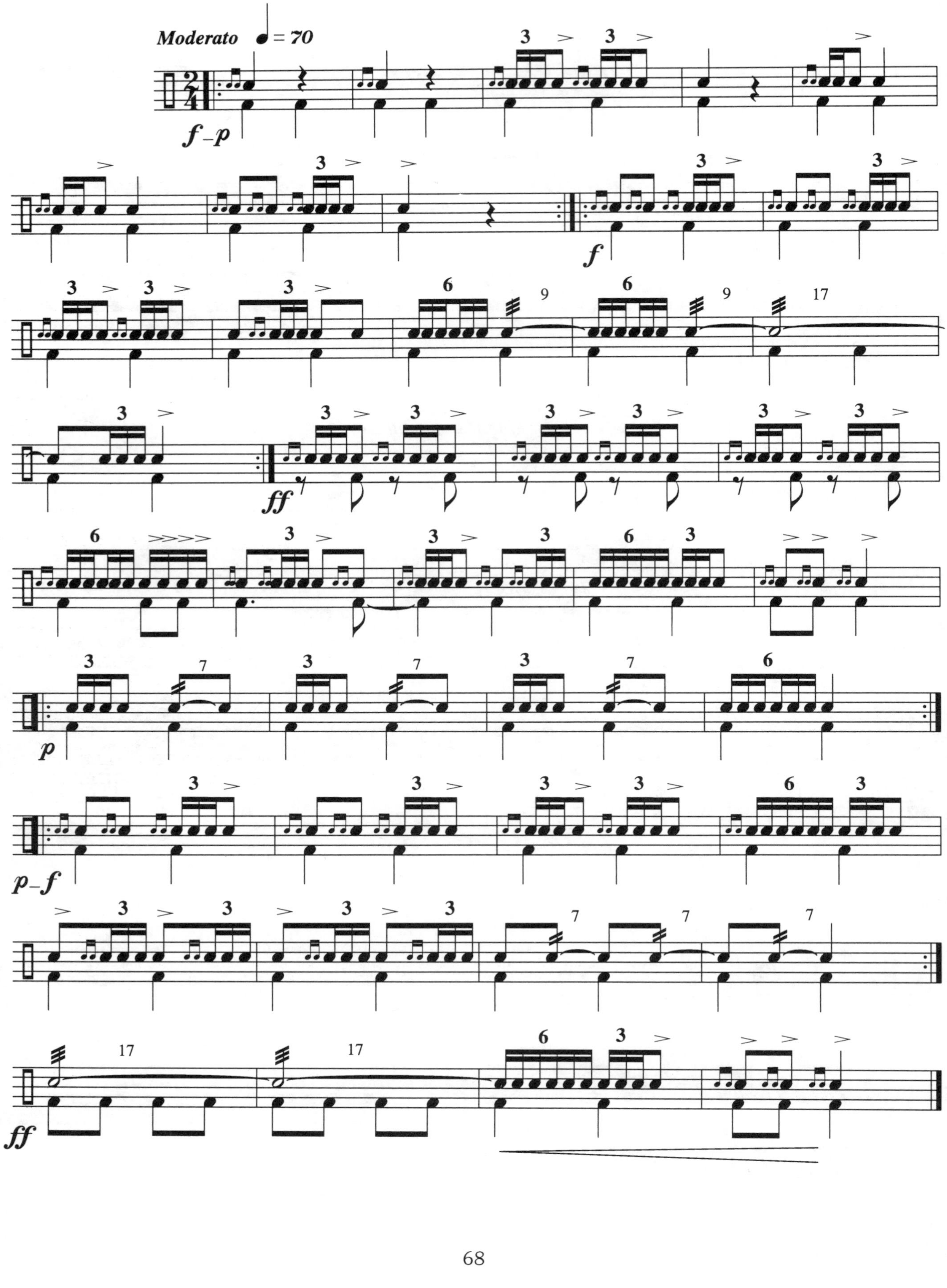

ETUDE NO. 22

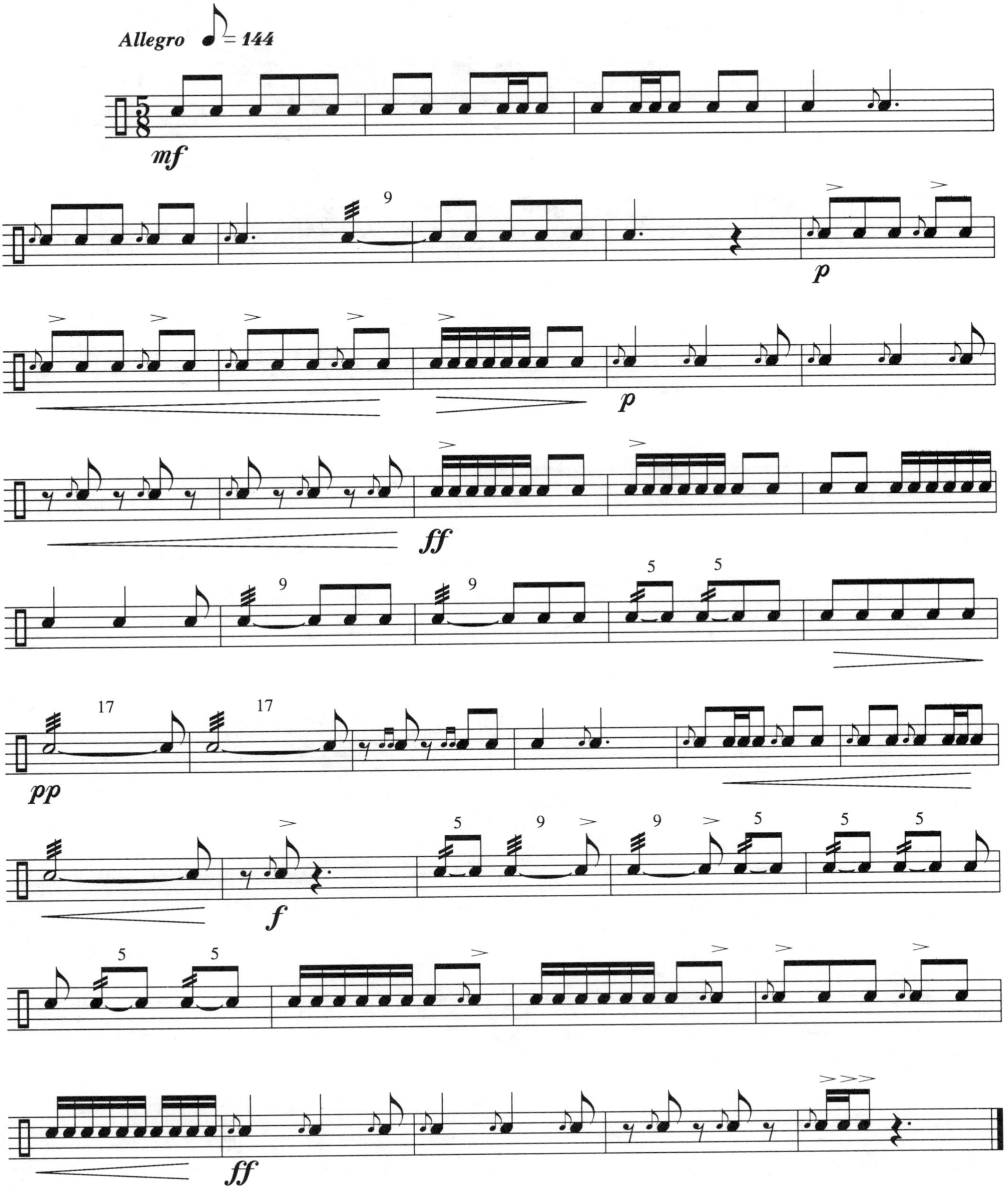

ETUDE NO. 23

LESSON 32

Drag Paradiddle No. 1

Drag Paradiddle No. 2

Single Drag Tap

Double Drag Tap

ETUDE NO. 24

The Orchestral Style Roll

The rolls presented thus far in this book are military or rudimental in style and are executed with a double bounce from each hand (RRLL). With the development of the symphony orchestra, and the concert or symphonic band in the nineteenth century, this type of roll did not suit many of the new styles of music. It became necessary for the snare drummer to produce a more refined, smoother sustained sound - a tone which was more complimentary to the sustained sound of string and woodwind instruments. This type of roll is produced by a very relaxed alternation of multiple bounces, hence the name *multiple bounce roll*, *buzz roll*, or *orchestral roll.*

It is important that the fulcrum be relaxed so the stick can buzz freely. Slight pressure from the middle finger will help propel the tip of the stick at the drum head. The ring and pinky fingers do not touch the stick and are used to lift the stick at the end of the roll.

Strive for an even sound from both hands. A multiple bounce roll can have anywhere from 4 to 6 bounces per hand. Practice the exercises below at a soft dynamic. Relaxation of the wrists, hands, arms, and <u>mind</u> are absolutely necessary. Repeat the exercises many times.

ETUDE NO. 25

= 200
ff
mp
ff
sub. p
(edge)
pp RRRRRRRR etc.
mp L (center)
(rim) mf
RL RL R LRL RLRLRLetc.
ff
R R R R R etc.
(edge)
pp L (center) mp
ff RL RL R LR LR L etc.
fff

ETUDE NO. 26

(all rolls are multiple bounce)

ETUDE NO. 27

ETUDE NO. 28

LESSON 34

"Lesson 25"

Six-Stroke Roll

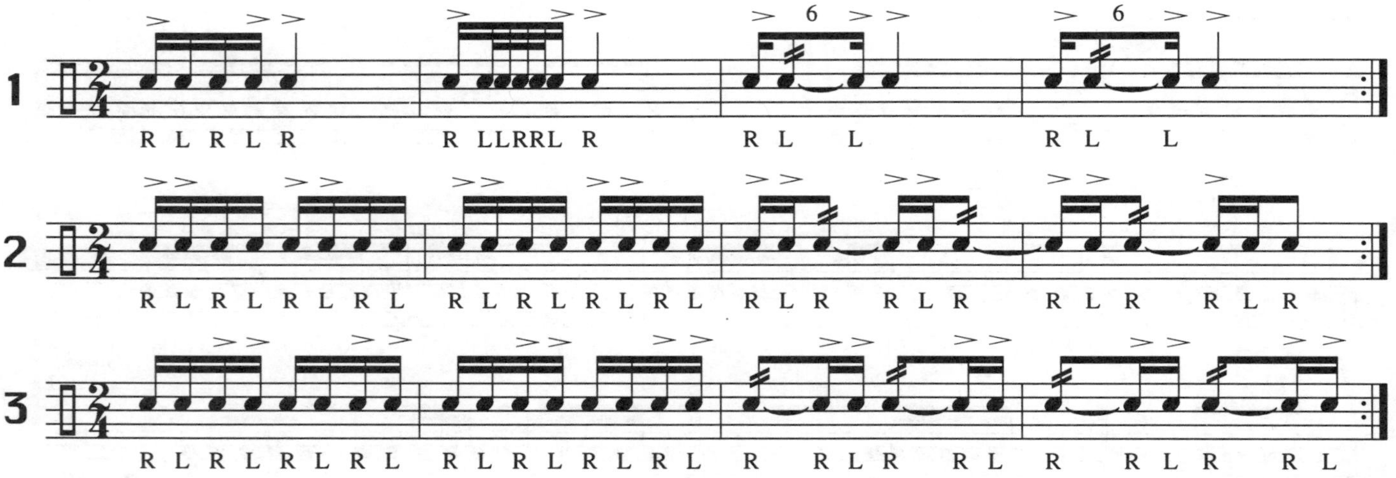

Ten-Stroke Roll

Inverted Flam Tap

Flam Drag

LESSON 35

Swiss Army Triplets

Pataflafla

Single Flammed Mill

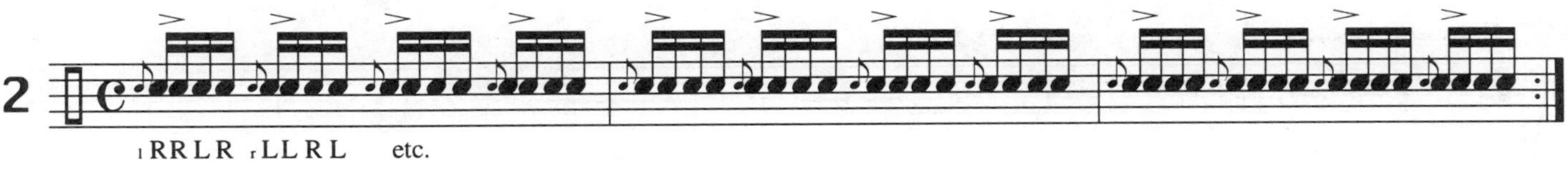

Single Dragadiddle

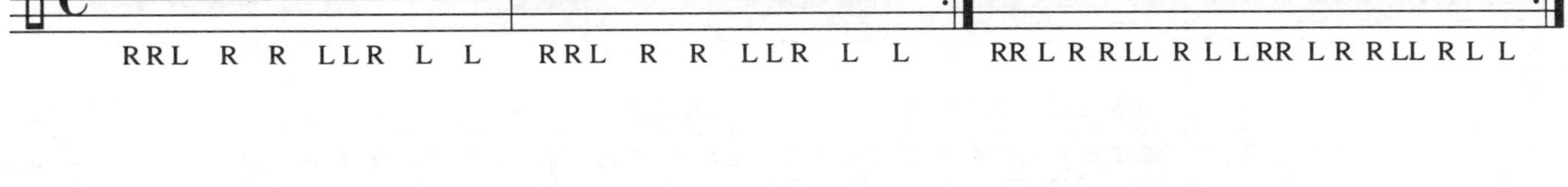

DUET NO. 1

Allegro ♩ = 100

pp
pp
mp
mp

DUET NO. 2

pp
pp
cres. poco a poco
cres. poco a poco
ff
ff
fp
fp

DUET NO. 3

Moderato ♩ = 84

ff
(rim)
(buzz)
fp

DUET NO. 4

p
mf
p
molto
p
molto
ff
ff
rim shots
on rim
fff
fff
p
p
sfz
sfz

FINAL ETUDE NO. 1

R R R R
L L R L R
orchestral buzz roll
rim shots
R R R L R L L L R L R R L R L R L R L L R L R R R R R
LRLR LRLR L R L R R L R R L R L L R L R
on rim
L R L R R L R R L R L L R L R
Turn snares off
R L R R L R L L R L R R L R L L R L R L R L R R R R
rim shots

FINAL ETUDE NO. 2

*play with one hand striking rim and head together

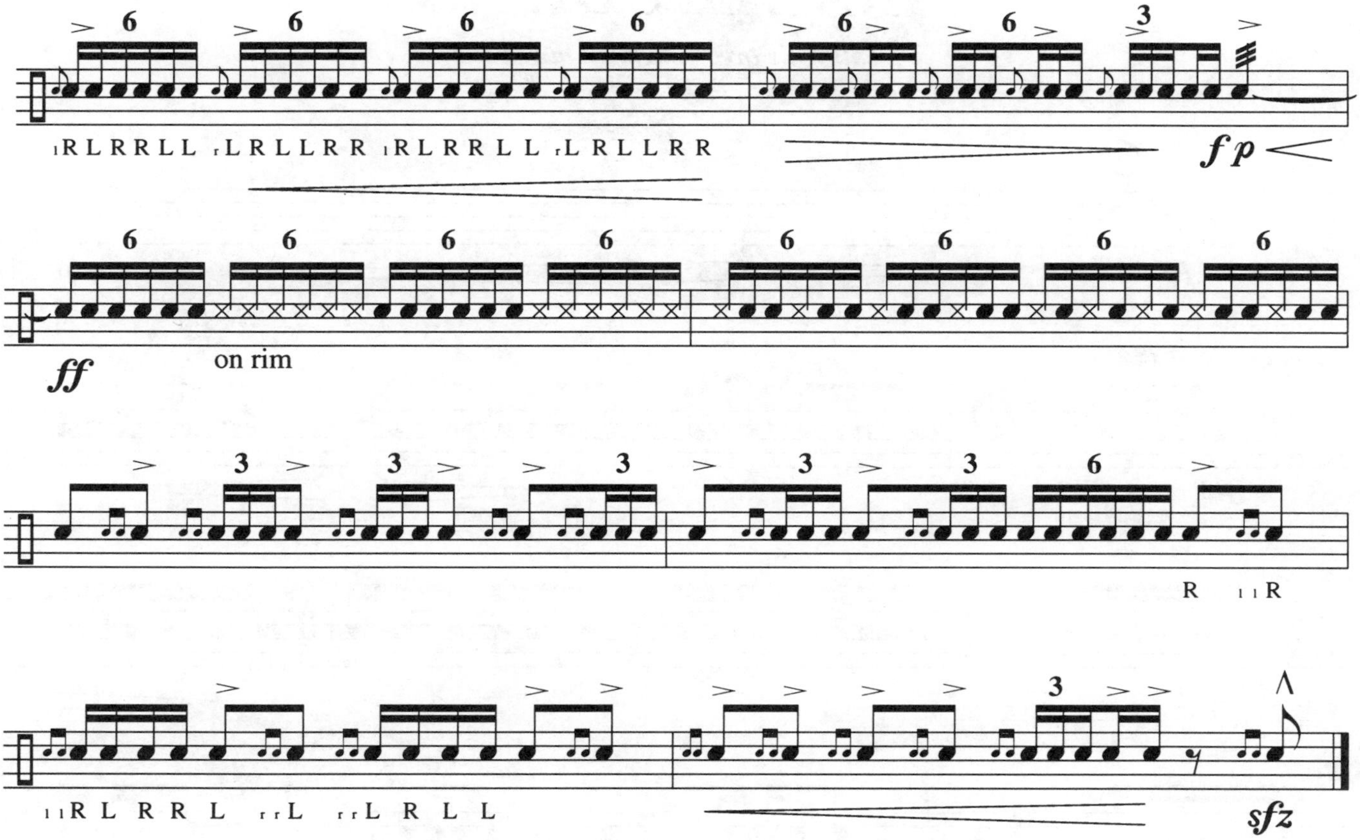
RLRRLL LRLLRR RLRRLL LRLLRR
fp
ff
on rim
R R
R L R R L L L R L L
sfz

FINAL ETUDE NO. 3

(all rolls are orchestral buzz rolls)

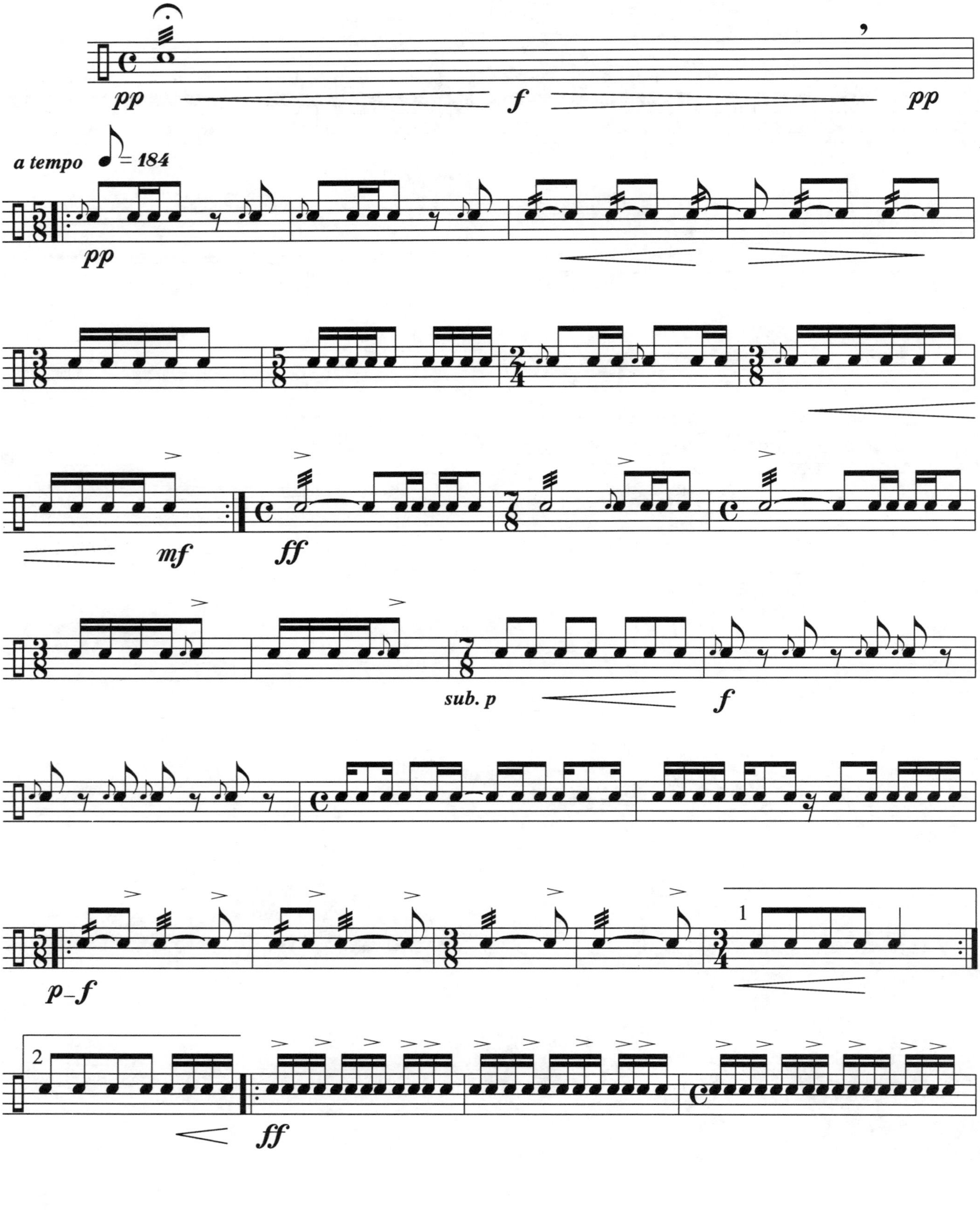

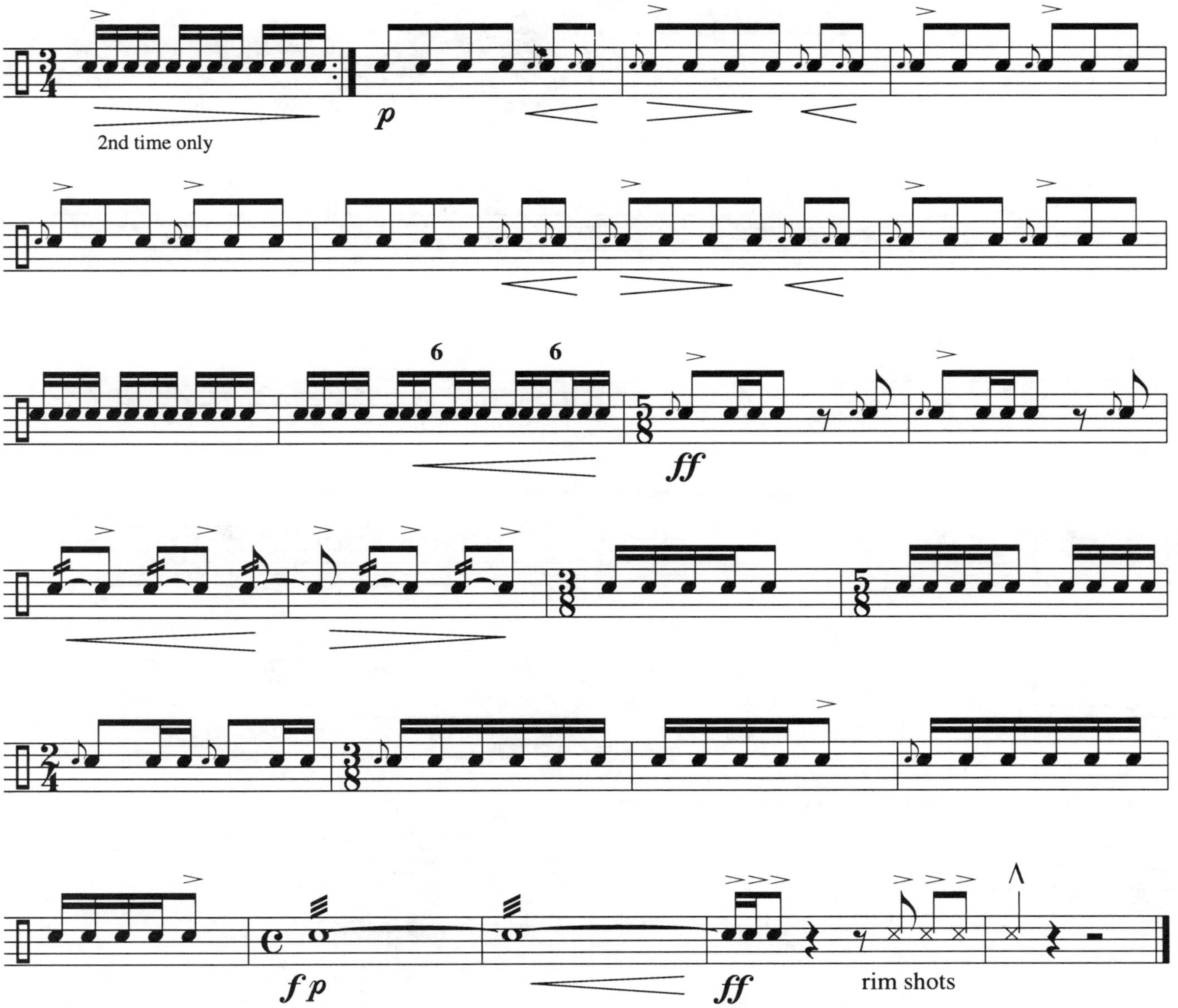
2nd time only
p
6
6
ff
fp
ff
rim shots

FINAL ETUDE NO. 4

*rim shot = right against left

*stick shot = one stick, butt in center, shaft against rim

FINAL ETUDE NO. 5

This etude should be played with a swing feel.
Dotted eighth-sixteenth rhythms are played with a triplet feel.

*rim shot=right stick on left

** hit right stick on left , allowing left stick to bounce on drum head.

*** rimshot= one stick hits rim and head simultaneously

RUDIMENT REVIEW

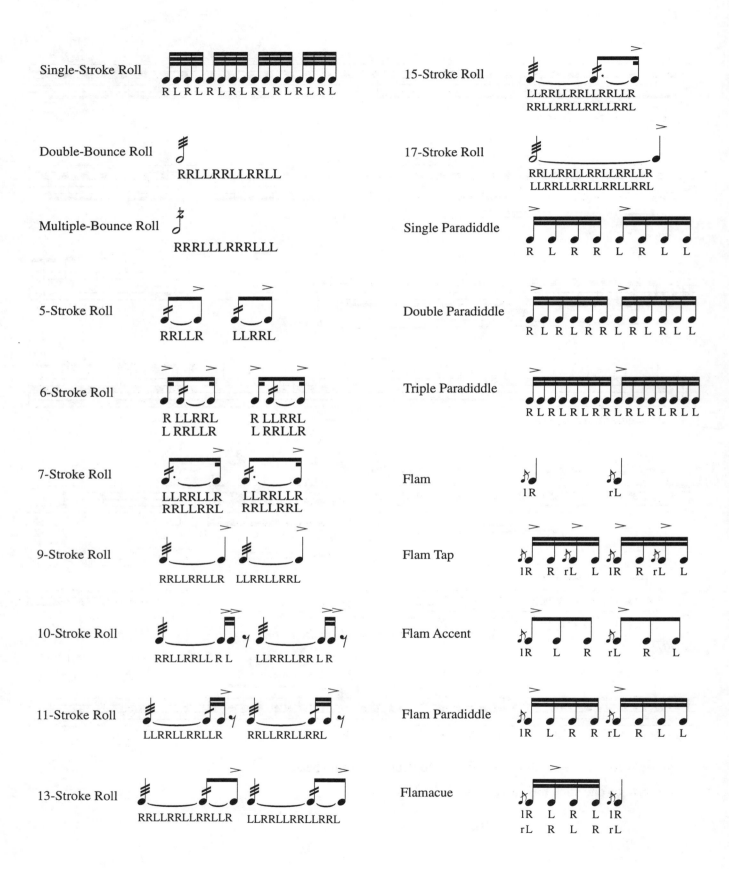

Single-Stroke Roll

R L R L R L R L R L R L R L R L

Double-Bounce Roll

RRLLRRLLRRLL

Multiple-Bounce Roll

RRRLLLRRRLLL

5-Stroke Roll

RRLLR LLRRL

6-Stroke Roll

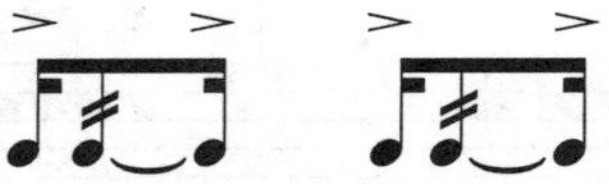

R LLRRL R LLRRL
L RRLLR L RRLLR

7-Stroke Roll

LLRRLLR LLRRLLR
RRLLRRL RRLLRRL

9-Stroke Roll

RRLLRRLLR LLRRLLRRL

10-Stroke Roll

RRLLRRLL R L LLRRLLRR L R

11-Stroke Roll

LLRRLLRRLLR RRLLRRLLRRL

13-Stroke Roll

RRLLRRLLRRLLR LLRRLLRRLLRRL

15-Stroke Roll

LLRRLLRRLLRRLLR
RRLLRRLLRRLLRRL

17-Stroke Roll

RRLLRRLLRRLLRRLLR
LLRRLLRRLLRRLLRRL

Single Paradiddle

R L R R L R L L

Double Paradiddle

R L R L R R L R L R L L

Triple Paradiddle

R L R L R L R R L R L R L R L L

Flam

lR rL

Flam Tap

lR R rL L lR R rL L

Flam Accent

lR L R rL R L

Flam Paradiddle

lR L R R rL R L L

Flamacue

lR L R L lR
rL R L R rL

Flam Paradiddle-Diddle

Inverted Flam Tap

Pataflafla

Swiss Army Triplets

Flam Drag

Dragadiddle

Drag

Single Tap Drag

Double Tap Drag

Lesson 25

Four-Stroke Ruff

Five-Stroke Ruff

Drag Paradiddle No. 1

Drag Paradiddle No. 2

Single Ratamacue

Double Ratamacue

Triple Ratamacue